Date Due

FE 2 '68			
MY			
MY 13			

by John Updike

THE
SAME DOOR

John Updike

THE
SAME DOOR

SHORT STORIES

Alfred A Knopf   New York

1963

...me in somewhat different
...hey were written
...ve here.

The lines by T. S. Eliot on the dedication page are quoted
from THE ELDER STATESMAN, copyright © 1959 by Thomas
Stearns Eliot, and used by permission of his publishers,
Farrar, Straus, and Cudahy.

L. C. Catalog card number: 59-9776

© John Updike, 1959

THIS IS A BORZOI BOOK,
PUBLISHED BY ALFRED A. KNOPF, INC.

PUBLISHED AUGUST 17, 1959
SECOND PRINTING, AUGUST 1963

TO MY PARENTS

And yet, how many of our present pleasures,
were we to examine them closely, would shrink
into nothing more than memories of past ones!
What would there be left of many of our emo-
tions, were we to reduce them to the exact quan-
tum of pure feeling they contain by subtracting
from them all that is merely reminiscence?

—BERGSON, LAUGHTER

But there's no vocabulary

For love within a family, love that's lived in
But not looked at, love within the light of which
All else is seen, the love within which
All other love finds speech.
This love is silent.

—T. S. ELIOT, THE ELDER STATESMAN

Contents

Contents

THE
SAME DOOR

Friends from Philadelphia

IN THE MOMENT BEFORE THE DOOR WAS OPENED TO HIM, he glimpsed her thigh below the half-drawn shade. Thelma was home, then. She was wearing the Camp Winniwoho T shirt and her quite short shorts.

"Why, my goodness: Janny!" she cried. She always pronounced his name, John, to rhyme with Ann. Earlier that vacation, she had visited in New York City, and tried to talk the way she thought they talked there. "What on earth ever brings you to me at this odd hour?"

"Hello, Thel," he said. "I hope—I guess this is a pretty bad time." She had been plucking her eyebrows again. He wished she wouldn't do that.

Thelma extended her arm and touched her fingers to the base of John's neck. It wasn't a fond gesture, just

a hostesslike one. "Now, Janny. You know that I—
my mother and I—are always happy to be seeing you.
Mother, who do you ever guess is here at this odd
hour?"

"Don't keep John standing there," Mrs. Lutz said.
Thelma's mother was settled in the deep red settee
watching television and smoking. A coffee cup being
used as an ashtray lay in her lap, and her dress was
hitched so that her knees showed.

"Hello, Mrs. Lutz," John said, trying not to look at
her broad, pale knees. "I really hate to bother you at
this odd hour."

"I don't see anything odd about it." She took a deep-
throated drag on her cigarette and exhaled through her
nostrils, the way men do. "Some of the other kids
were here earlier this afternoon."

"I would have come in if anybody had told me."

Thelma said, "Oh, Janny! Stop trying to make a
martyr of yourself. Keep in touch, they say, if you
want to keep up."

He felt his face grow hot and knew he was blushing,
which made him blush all the more. Mrs. Lutz shook a
wrinkled pack of Herbert Tareytons at him. "Smoke?"
she said.

"I guess not, thanks a lot."

"You've stopped? It's a bad habit. I wish I had
stopped at your age. I'm not sure I even *begun* at your
age."

"No, it's just that I have to go home soon, and my
mother would smell the smoke on my breath. She can
smell it even through chewing gum."

"Why must you go home soon?" Thelma asked.

Mrs. Lutz sniffled. "I have sinus. I can't even smell the flowers in the garden or the food on the table any more. Let the kids smoke if they want, if it makes them feel better. I don't care. My Thelma, she can smoke right in her own home, her own living room, if she wants to. But she doesn't seem to have the taste for it. I'm just as glad, to tell the truth."

John hated interrupting, but it was close to five-thirty. "I have a problem," he said.

"A problem—how gruesome," Thelma said. "And here I thought, Mother, I was being favored with a social call."

"Don't talk like that," Mrs. Lutz said.

"It's sort of complex," John began.

"Talk like what, Mother? Talk like what?"

"Then let me turn this off," Mrs. Lutz said, snapping the right knob on the television set.

"Oh, Mother, and I was listening to it!" Thelma toppled into a chair, her legs flashing. John thought when she pouted, she was delicious.

Mrs. Lutz had set herself to give sympathy. Her lap was broadened and her hands were laid palm upward in it.

"It's not much of a problem," John assured her. "But we're having some people up from Philadelphia." He turned to Thelma and added, "If anything is going on tonight, I can't get out."

"Life is just too, too full of disappointments," Thelma said.

"Look, is there?"

: 5 :

"Too, too full," Thelma said.

Mrs. Lutz made fluttery motions out of her lap. "These Philadelphia people."

John said, "Maybe I shouldn't bother you about this." He waited, but she just looked more and more patient, so he went on. "My mother wants to give them wine, and my father isn't home from school yet. He might not get home before the liquor store closes. It's at six, isn't it? My mother's busy cleaning, so I walked in."

"She made you walk the whole mile? Poor thing, can't you drive?" Mrs. Lutz asked.

"*Sure* I can drive. But I'm not sixteen yet."

"You look a lot taller than sixteen."

John looked at Thelma to see how she took that one, but Thelma was pretending to read a rented novel wrapped in cellophane.

"I walked all the way in to the liquor store," John told Mrs. Lutz, "but they wouldn't give me anything without written permission. It was a new man."

"Your sorrow has rent me in twain," Thelma said, as if she was reading it from the book.

"Pay no attention, Johnny," Mrs. Lutz said. "Now Frank will be home any time. Why not wait until he comes and let him run down with you for a bottle?"

"That sounds wonderful. Thanks an awful lot, really."

Mrs. Lutz's hand descended upon the television knob. Some smiling man was playing the piano. John didn't know who he was; there wasn't any television at his house. They watched in silence until Mr. Lutz thumped on the porch outside. The empty milk bottles tinkled, as if they had been nudged. "Now don't be surprised if he has a bit of a load on," Mrs. Lutz said.

Actually, he didn't act at all drunk. He was like a happy husband in the movies. He called Thelma his little pookie-pie and kissed her on the forehead; then he called his wife his big pookie-pie and kissed her on the mouth. Then he solemnly shook John's hand and told him how very, very happy he was to see him here and asked after his parents. "Is that goon still on television?" he said finally.

"Daddy, please pay attention to somebody else," Thelma said, turning off the television set. "Janny wants to talk to you."

"And *I* want to talk to *Johnny*," Thelma's father said. He spread his arms suddenly, clenching and un-clenching his fists. He was a big man, with shaved gray hair above his tiny ears. John couldn't think of the word to begin.

Mrs. Lutz explained the errand. When she was through, Mr. Lutz said, "People from Philadelphia. I bet their name isn't William L. Trexler, is it?"

"No. I forget their name, but it's not that. The man is an engineer. The woman went to college with my mother."

"Oh. College people. Then we must get them something very, very nice, I should say."

"Daddy," Thelma said. "*Please*. The store will close."

"Tessie, you hear John. People from college. People with diplomas. And it is very nearly closing time, and who isn't on their way?" He took John's shoulder in one hand and Thelma's arm in the other and hustled them through the door. "We'll be back in one minute, Mamma," he said.

"Drive carefully," Mrs. Lutz said from the shadowed porch.

Mr. Lutz drove a huge blue Buick. "I never went to college," he said, "yet I buy a new car whenever I want." His tone wasn't nasty, but soft and full of wonder.

"Oh, Daddy, not *this* again," Thelma said, shaking her head at John, so he could understand what all she had to go through. When she looks like that, John thought, I could bite her lip until it bleeds.

"Ever driven this kind of car, John?" Mr. Lutz asked.

"No. The only thing I can drive is my parents' Plymouth, and that not very well."

"What year car is it?"

"I don't know exactly." John knew perfectly well it was a 1947 model. "We got it long after the war. It has a gear shift. This is automatic, isn't it?"

"Automatic shift, fluid transmission, directional lights, the works," Mr. Lutz said. "Now, isn't it funny, John? Here is your father, an educated man, with an old Plymouth, yet at the same time I, who never read more than twenty, thirty books in my life . . . . it doesn't seem as if there's justice." He slapped the fender, bent over to get into the car, straightened up abruptly, and said, "Do you want to drive it?"

Thelma said, "Daddy's asking you something."

"I don't know how," John said.

"It's very easy to learn, very easy. You just slide in there—come on, it's getting late." John got in on the driver's side. He peered out of the windshield. It was a wider car than the Plymouth; the hood looked wide as a boat.

Mr. Lutz asked him to grip the little lever behind the steering wheel. "You pull it toward you like *that*, that's it, and fit it into one of these notches. 'P' stands for 'parking'—I hardly ever use that one. 'N,' that's 'neutral,' like on the car you have, 'D' means 'drive'— just put it in there and the car does all the work for you. You are using that one ninety-nine per cent of the time. 'L' is 'low,' for very steep hills, going up or down. And 'R' stands for—what?"

"Reverse," John said.

"Very, very good. Tessie, he's a smart boy. He'll never own a new car. And when you put them all together, you can remember their order by the sentence, Paint No Dimes Light Red. I thought that up when I was teaching my oldest girl how to drive."

"Paint No Dimes Light Red," John said.

"Excellent. Now, let's go."

A bubble was developing in John's stomach. "What gear do you want it in to start?" he asked Mr. Lutz.

Mr. Lutz must not have heard him, because all he said was "Let's go" again, and he drummed on the dashboard with his fingertips. They were thick, square, furry fingers.

Thelma leaned up from the back seat. Her cheek almost touched John's ear. She whispered, "Put it at 'D.'"

He did, then he looked for the starter. "How does he start it?" he asked Thelma.

"I never watch him," she said. "There was a button in the last car, but I don't see it in this one."

"Push on the pedal," Mr. Lutz sang, staring straight

ahead and smiling, "and away we go. And ah, ah, waay we go."

"Just step on the gas," Thelma suggested. John pushed down firmly, to keep his leg from trembling. The motor roared and the car bounded away from the curb. Within a block, though, he could manage the car pretty well.

"It rides like a boat on smooth water," he told his two passengers. The metaphor pleased him.

Mr. Lutz squinted ahead. "Like a what?"

"Like a boat."

"Don't go so fast," Thelma said.

"The motor's so quiet," John explained. "Like a sleeping cat."

Without warning, a truck pulled out of Pearl Street. Mr. Lutz, trying to brake, stamped his foot on the empty floor in front of him. John could hardly keep from laughing. "I see him," he said, easing his speed so that the truck had just enough room to make its turn. "Those trucks think they own the road," he said. He let one hand slide away from the steering wheel. One-handed, he whipped around a bus. "What'll she do on the open road?"

"That's a good question, John," Mr. Lutz said. "And I don't know the answer. Eighty, maybe."

"The speedometer goes up to a hundred and ten." Another pause—nobody seemed to be talking. John said, "Hell. A baby could drive one of these."

"For instance, you," Thelma said. That meant she had noticed how well he was driving.

There were a lot of cars at the liquor store, so John had to double-park the big Buick. "That's close enough, close enough," Mr. Lutz said. "Don't get any closer, whoa!" He was out of the car before John could bring it to a complete stop. "You and Tessie wait here," he said. "I'll go in for the liquor."

"Mr. Lutz. Say, Mr. Lutz," John called.

"Daddy!" Thelma shouted.

Mr. Lutz returned. "What is it, boys and girls?" His tone, John noticed, was becoming reedy. He was probably getting hungry.

"Here's the money they gave me." John pulled two wadded dollars from the change pocket of his dungarees. "My mother said to get something inexpensive but nice."

"Inexpensive but nice?" Mr. Lutz repeated.

"She said something about California sherry."

"What did she say about it? To get it? Or not to?"

"I guess to get it."

"You guess." Mr. Lutz shoved himself away from the car and walked backward toward the store as he talked. "You and Tessie wait in the car. Don't go off somewhere. It's getting late. I'll be only one minute."

John leaned back in his seat and gracefully rested one hand at the top of the steering wheel. "I like your father."

"You don't know how he acts to Mother," Thelma said.

John studied the clean line under his wrist and thumb. He flexed his wrist and watched the neat little muscles move in his forearm. "You know what I need?" he said. "A wristwatch."

"Oh, Jan," Thelma said. "Stop admiring your own hand. It's really disgusting."

A ghost of a smile flickered over his lips, but he let his strong nervous fingers remain as they were. "I'd sell my soul for a drag right now."

"Daddy keeps a pack in the glove compartment," Thelma said. "I'd get them if my fingernails weren't so long."

"*I'll* get it open," John said. He did. They fished one cigarette out of the old pack they found and took alternate puffs. "Ah," John said, "that first drag of the day, clawing and scraping its way down your throat."

"Be on the lookout for Daddy. They hate my smoking."

"Thelma."

"Yes?" She stared deep into his eyes, her face half hidden in blue shadow.

"Don't pluck your eyebrows."

"I think it looks nice."

"It's like calling me 'Jan.' " There was a silence, not awkward.

"Get rid of the rette, Jan. Daddy just passed the window."

Being in the liquor store had put Mr. Lutz in a soberer mood. "Here you be, John," he said, in a businesslike way. He handed John a tall, velvet-red bottle. "Better let me drive. You drive like a veteran, but I know the roads."

"I can walk from your house, Mr. Lutz," John said, knowing Mr. Lutz wouldn't make him walk. "Thanks an awful lot for all you've done."

"I'll drive you up. Philadelphians can't be kept waiting. We can't make this young man walk a mile, now can we, Tessie?" Nobody knew what to say to this last remark, so they kept quiet all the way, although several things were bothering John.

When the car stopped in front of his house, he forced himself to ask, "Say, Mr. Lutz. I wonder if there was any change?"

"What? Oh. I nearly forgot. You'll have your daddy thinking I'm a crook." He reached into his pocket and without looking handed John a dollar, a quarter, and a penny.

"This seems like a lot," John said. The wine must be cheap. Maybe he should have let his mother buy it, like she had wanted to.

"It's your change," Mr. Lutz said.

"Well, thanks an awful lot."

"Goodbye now," Mr. Lutz said.

"So long." John slammed the door. "Goodbye, Thelma. Don't forget what I told you." He winked.

The car pulled out, and John walked up the path. "Don't forget what I told you," he repeated to himself, winking. The bottle was cool and heavy in his hands. He glanced at the label, which read "Château Mouton-Rothschild 1937."

Ace in the Hole

THE MOMENT HIS CAR TOUCHED THE BOULEVARD HEAD-
ing home, Ace flicked on the radio. He needed the
radio, especially today. In the seconds before the tubes
warmed up, he said aloud, doing it just to hear a human voice, "Jesus. She'll pop her lid." His voice,
though familiar, irked him; it sounded thin and
scratchy, as if the bones in his head were picking up
static. In a deeper register Ace added, "She'll murder
me." Then the radio came on, warm and strong, so he
stopped worrying. The Five Kings were doing "Blueberry Hill"; to hear them made Ace feel so sure inside
that from the pack pinched between the car roof and
the sun shield he plucked a cigarette, hung it on his
lower lip, snapped a match across the rusty place on
the dash, held the flame in the instinctive spot near
the tip of his nose, dragged, and blew out the match,
all in time to the music. He rolled down the window

and snapped the match so it spun end over end into the gutter. "Two points," he said, and cocked the cigarette toward the roof of the car, sucked powerfully, and exhaled two plumes through his nostrils. He was beginning to feel like himself, Ace Anderson, for the first time that whole day, a bad day. He beat time on the accelerator. The car jerked crazily. "On Blueberry Hill," he sang, "my heart stood still. The wind in the wil-low tree"—he braked for a red light—"played love's suh-*weet* melodee—"

"Go, Dad, bust your lungs!" a kid's voice blared. The kid was riding in a '52 Pontiac that had pulled up beside Ace at the light. The profile of the driver, another kid, was dark over his shoulder.

Ace looked over at him and smiled slowly, just letting one side of his mouth lift a little. "Ram it," he said, good-naturedly. It was only a couple of years since he had been their age.

But the kid, who looked Greek, lifted his thick upper lip and spat out the window. The spit gleamed on the asphalt like a half-dollar.

"Now isn't that pretty?" Ace said, keeping one eye on the light. "You miserable wop. You are *mis*erable." While the kid was trying to think of some smart comeback, the light changed. Ace dug out so hard he smelled burned rubber. In his rear-view mirror he saw the Pontiac lurch forward a few yards, then stop dead, right in the middle of the intersection.

The idea of them stalling their fat tin Pontiac kept him in a good humor all the way home. He decided to stop at his mother's place and pick up the baby, instead of waiting for Evey to do it. His mother must have seen him drive up. She came out on the porch holding a plastic spoon and smelling of cake.

"You're out early," she told him.

"Friedman fired me," Ace told her.

"Good for you," his mother said. "I always said he never treated you right." She brought a cigarette out of her apron pocket and tucked it deep into one corner of her mouth, the way she did when something pleased her.

Ace lighted it for her. "Friedman was O.K. personally," he said. "He just wanted too much for his money. I didn't mind working Saturdays, but until eleven, twelve Friday nights was too much. Everybody has a right to some leisure."

"Well, I don't dare think what Evey will say, but I, for one, thank dear God you had the brains to get out of it. I always said that job had no future to it—no future of any kind, Freddy."

"I guess," Ace admitted. "But I wanted to keep at it, for the family's sake."

"Now, I know I shouldn't be saying this, but any time Evey—this is just between us—any time Evey thinks she can do better, there's room for you *and* Bonnie right in your father's house." She pinched her lips together. He could almost hear the old lady think, There, I've said it.

"Look, Mom, Evey tries awfully hard, and anyway you know she can't work that way. Not that *that*—I mean, she's a realist, too . . ." He let the rest of the thought fade as he watched a kid across the street dribbling a basketball around a telephone pole that had a backboard and net nailed on it.

"Evey's a wonderful girl of her own kind. But I've always said, and your father agrees, Roman Catholics ought to marry among themselves. Now I know I've said it before, but when they get out in the greater world—"

"*No*, Mom."

She frowned, smoothed herself, and said, "Your name was in the paper today."

Ace chose to let that go by. He kept watching the kid with the basketball. It was funny how, though the whole point was to get the ball up into the air, kids grabbed it by the sides and squeezed. Kids just didn't think.

"Did you hear?" his mother asked.

"Sure, but so what?" Ace said. His mother's lower lip was coming at him, so he changed the subject. "I guess I'll take Bonnie."

His mother went into the house and brought back his daughter, wrapped in a blue blanket. The baby looked dopey. "She fussed all day," his mother complained. "I said to your father, 'Bonnie is a dear little girl, but without a doubt she's her mother's daughter.' You were the best-natured boy."

"Well I *had* everything," Ace said with impatience. His mother blinked like an owl. He nicely dropped his cigarette into a brown flowerpot on the edge of the porch and took his daughter into his arms. She was getting heavier, solid. When he reached the end of the cement walk, his mother was still on the porch, waving to him. He was so close he could see the fat around her elbow jiggle, and he only lived a half block up the street, yet here she was, waving to him as if he was going to Japan.

At the door of his car, it seemed stupid to him to drive the measly half block home. "Never ride where you can walk," Coach Behn used to tell his boys. Ace left the ignition keys in his pocket and ran along the pavement with Bonnie laughing and bouncing at his chest. He slammed the door of his landlady's house open and shut, pounded up the two flights of stairs, and was panting so hard when he reached the door of his apartment that it took him a couple of seconds to fit the key into the lock.

The run must have tuned Bonnie up. As soon as he lowered her into the crib, she began to shout and wave her arms. He didn't want to play with her. He tossed some blocks and a rattle into the crib and walked into the bathroom, where he turned on the hot water and began to comb his hair. Holding the comb under the faucet before every stroke, he combed his hair forward. It was so long, one strand curled under his nose and touched his lips. He whipped the whole mass back with a single pull. He tucked in the tufts around his ears, and ran the comb straight back on both sides of his head. With his fingers he felt for the little ridge at the back where the two sides met. It was there, as it should have been. Finally, he mussed the hair in front enough for one little lock to droop over his forehead, like Alan Ladd. It made the temple seem lower than it was. Every day, his hairline looked higher. He had observed all around him how blond men went bald first.

He remembered reading somewhere, though, that baldness shows virility.

On his way to the kitchen he flipped the left-hand knob of the television. Bonnie was always quieter with the set on. Ace didn't see how she could understand much of it, but it seemed to mean something to her. He found a can of beer in the refrigerator behind some brownish lettuce and those hot dogs Evey never got around to cooking. She'd be home any time. The clock said 5:12. She'd pop her lid.

Ace didn't see what he could do but try and reason with her. "Evey," he'd say, "you ought to thank God I got out of it. It had no future to it at all." He hoped she wouldn't get too mad, because when she was mad he wondered if he should have married her, and doubting that made him feel crowded. It was bad enough, his mother always crowding him. He punched the two triangles in the top of the beer can, the little triangle first, and then the big one, the one he drank from. He hoped Evey wouldn't say anything that couldn't be forgotten. What women didn't seem to realize was that there were things you knew but shouldn't say.

He felt sorry he had called the kid in the car a wop.

Ace balanced the beer on a corner where two rails of the crib met and looked under the chairs for the morning paper. He had trouble finding his name, because it was at the bottom of a column on an inside sports page, in a small article about the county basketball statistics:

"Dusty" Tremwick, Grosvenor Park's sure-fingered center, copped the individual scoring honors with a season's grand (and we do mean grand) total of

376 points. This is within eighteen points of the all-time record of 394 racked up in the 1949–1950 season by Olinger High's Fred Anderson.

Ace angrily sailed the paper into an armchair. Now it was Fred Anderson; it used to be Ace. He hated being called Fred, especially in print, but then the sportswriters were all office boys anyway, Behn used to say.

"Do not just ask for shoe polish," a man on television said, "but ask for *Emu Shoe Gloss,* the *only* polish that absolutely *guarantees* to make your shoes look shinier than new." Ace turned the sound off, so that the man moved his mouth like a fish blowing bubbles. Right away, Bonnie howled, so Ace turned it up loud enough to drown her out and went into the kitchen, without knowing what he wanted there. He wasn't hungry; his stomach was tight. It used to be like that when he walked to the gymnasium alone in the dark before a game and could see the people from town, kids and parents, crowding in at the lighted doors. But once he was inside, the locker room would be bright and hot, and the other guys would be there, laughing and towel-slapping, and the tight feeling would leave. Now there were whole days when it didn't leave.

A key scratched at the door lock. Ace decided to stay in the kitchen. Let *her* find *him.* Her heels clicked on the floor for a step or two; then the television set went off. Bonnie began to cry. "Shut up, honey," Evey said. There was a silence.

"I'm home," Ace called.

"No kidding. I thought Bonnie got the beer by herself."

Ace laughed. She was in a sarcastic mood, thinking she was Lauren Bacall. That was all right, just so she kept funny. Still smiling, Ace eased into the living room and got hit with, "What are *you* smirking about? Another question: What's the idea running up the street with Bonnie like she was a football?"

"You saw that?"

"Your mother told me."

"You saw her?"

"Of course I saw her. I dropped by to pick up Bonnie. What the hell do you think?—I read her tiny mind?"

"Take it easy," Ace said, wondering if Mom had told her about Friedman.

"Take it easy? Don't coach *me*. Another question: Why's the car out in front of her place? You give the car to her?"

"Look, I parked it there to pick up Bonnie, and I thought I'd leave it there."

"Why?"

"What do you mean, why? I just did. I just thought I'd walk. It's not that far, you know."

"No, I don't know. If you'd be on your feet all day a block would look like one hell of a long way."

"Okay. I'm sorry."

She hung up her coat and stepped out of her shoes and walked around the room picking up things. She stuck the newspaper in the wastebasket.

Ace said, "My name was in the paper today."

"They spell it right?" She shoved the paper deep into the basket with her foot. There was no doubt; she knew about Friedman.

"They called me Fred."

"Isn't that your name? What *is* your name anyway? Hero J. Great?"

There wasn't any answer, so Ace didn't try any. He sat down on the sofa, lighted a cigarette, and waited.

Evey picked up Bonnie. "Poor thing stinks. What does your mother do, scrub out the toilet with her?"

"Can't you take it easy? I know you're tired."

"You should. I'm always tired."

Evey and Bonnie went into the bathroom; when they came out, Bonnie was clean and Evey was calm. Evey sat down in an easy chair beside Ace and rested her stocking feet on his knees. "Hit me," she said, twiddling her fingers for the cigarette.

The baby crawled up to her chair and tried to stand, to see what he gave her. Leaning over close to Bonnie's nose, Evey grinned, smoke leaking through her teeth, and said, "Only for grownups, honey."

"Eve," Ace began, "there was no future in that job. Working all Saturday, and then Friday nights on top of it."

"I know. Your mother told *me* all that, too. All I want from you is what happened."

She was going to take it like a sport, then. He tried to remember how it *did* happen. "It wasn't my fault," he said. "Friedman told me to back this '51 Chevvy into the line that faces Church Street. He just bought it from an old guy this morning who said it only had thirteen thousand on it. So in I jump and start her up. There was a knock in the engine like a machine gun. I almost told Friedman he'd bought a squirrel, but you know I cut that smart stuff out ever since Palotta laid me off."

"You told me that story. What happens in this one?"

"Look, Eve. I *am* telling ya. Do you want me to go out to a movie or something?"

"Suit yourself."

"So I jump in the Chevvy and snap it back in line, and there was a kind of scrape and thump. I get out and look and Friedman's running over, his arms going like *this*"—Ace whirled his own arms and laughed—"and here was the whole back fender of a '49 Merc mashed in. Just looked like somebody took a planer and shaved off the bulge, you know, there at the back." He tried to show her with his hands. "The Chevvy, though, didn't have a dent. It even gained some paint. But *Friedman*, to *hear* him—Boy, they can rave when their pocketbook's hit. He said"—Ace laughed again—"never mind."

Evey said, "You're proud of yourself."

"No, listen. I'm not happy about it. But there wasn't a thing I could *do*. It wasn't my driving at all. I looked over on the other side, and there was just two or three inches between the Chevvy and a Buick. *Nobody* could have gotten into that hole. Even if it had hair on it." He thought this was pretty good.

She didn't. "You could have looked."

"There just wasn't the *space*. Friedman said stick it in; I stuck it in."

"But you could have looked and moved the other cars to make more room."

"I guess that would have been the smart thing."

"I guess, too. Now what?"

"What do you mean?"

"I mean now what? Are you going to give up? Go back to the Army? Your mother? Be a basketball pro? What?"

"You know I'm not tall enough. Anybody under six-six they don't want."

"Is that so? Six-six? Well, please listen to this, Mr. Six-Foot-Five-and-a-Half: I'm fed up. I'm ready as Christ to let you run." She stabbed her cigarette into an ashtray on the arm of the chair so hard the ashtray jumped to the floor. Evey flushed and shut up.

What Ace hated most in their arguments was these silences after Evey had said something so ugly she wanted to take it back. "Better ask the priest first," he murmured.

She sat right up. "If there's one thing I don't want to hear about from you it's priests. You let the priests to me. You don't know a damn thing about it. Not a damn thing."

"Hey, look at Bonnie," he said, trying to make his tone easy.

Evey didn't hear him. "If you think," she went on, "if for one rotten moment you think, Mr. Fred, that the be-all and end-all of my life is you and your hot-shot stunts—"

"Look, Mother," Ace pleaded, pointing at Bonnie. The baby had picked up the ashtray and put it on her head for a hat.

Evey glanced down angrily. "Cute," she said. "Cute as her daddy."

The ashtray slid from Bonnie's head and she groped after it.

"Yeah, but watch," Ace said. "Watch her hands. They're sure."

"You're nuts," Evey said.

"No, honest. Bonnie's great. She's a natural. Get the rattle for her. Never mind, I'll get it." In two steps, Ace was at Bonnie's crib, picking the rattle out of the mess of blocks and plastic rings and beanbags. He extended the rattle toward his daughter, shaking it delicately. Made wary by this burst of attention, Bonnie reached with both hands; like two separate animals they approached from opposite sides and touched the smooth rattle simultaneously. A smile worked up on her face. Ace tugged weakly. She held on, and then tugged back. "She's a natural," Ace said, "and it won't do her any good because she's a girl. Baby, we got to have a boy."

"I'm not your baby," Evey said, closing her eyes.

Saying "Baby" over and over again, Ace backed up to the radio and, without turning around, manipulated the volume knob. In the moment before the tubes warmed up, Evey had time to say, "Wise up, Freddy. What shall we do?"

The radio came in on something slow: dinner music. Ace picked Bonnie up and set her in the crib. "Shall we dance?" he asked his wife, bowing.

"I want to talk."

"Baby. It's the cocktail hour."

"This is getting us no place," she said, rising from her chair, though.

"Fred Junior. I can see him now," he said, seeing nothing.

"We will have no Juniors."

In her crib, Bonnie whimpered at the sight of her mother being seized. Ace fitted his hand into the natural place on Evey's back and she shuffled stiffly into his lead. When, with a sudden injection of saxophones, the tempo quickened, he spun her out carefully, keeping the beat with his shoulders. Her hair brushed his lips as she minced in, then swung away, to the end of his arm; he could feel her toes dig into the carpet. He flipped his own hair back from his eyes. The music ate through his skin and mixed with the nerves and small veins; he seemed to be great again, and all the other kids were around them, in a ring, clapping time.

Tomorrow and Tomorrow and So Forth

WHIRLING, TALKING, 11D BEGAN TO ENTER ROOM 109. From the quality of their excitement Mark Prosser guessed it would rain. He had been teaching high school for three years, yet his students still impressed him; they were such sensitive animals. They reacted so infallibly to merely barometric pressure.

In the doorway, Brute Young paused while little Barry Snyder giggled at his elbow. Barry's stagy laugh rose and fell, dipping down toward some vile secret that had to be tasted and retasted, then soaring artificially to proclaim that he, little Barry, shared such a secret with the school's fullback. Being Brute's stooge was precious to Barry. The fullback paid no attention to him; he twisted his neck to stare at something not yet coming through the door. He yielded heavily to the procession pressing him forward.

Right under Prosser's eyes, like a murder suddenly appearing in an annalistic frieze of kings and queens, someone stabbed a girl in the back with a pencil. She ignored the assault saucily. Another hand yanked out Geoffrey Langer's shirt-tail. Geoffrey, a bright student, was uncertain whether to laugh it off or defend himself with anger, and made a weak, half-turning gesture of compromise, wearing an expression of distant arrogance that Prosser instantly coördinated with feelings of fear he used to have. All along the line, in the glitter of key chains and the acute angles of turned-back shirt cuffs, an electricity was expressed which simple weather couldn't generate.

Mark wondered if today Gloria Angstrom wore that sweater, an ember-pink angora, with very brief sleeves. The virtual sleevelessness was the disturbing factor: the exposure of those two serene arms to the air, white as thighs against the delicate wool.

His guess was correct. A vivid pink patch flashed through the jiggle of arms and shoulders as the final knot of youngsters entered the room.

"Take your seats," Mr. Prosser said. "Come on. Let's go."

Most obeyed, but Peter Forrester, who had been at the center of the group around Gloria, still lingered in the doorway with her, finishing some story, apparently determined to make her laugh or gasp. When she did gasp, he tossed his head with satisfaction. His orange hair bobbed. Redheads are all alike, Mark thought, with their white eyelashes and pale puffy faces and thyroid eyes, their mouths always twisted with preposterous self-confidence. Bluffers, the whole bunch.

When Gloria, moving in a considered, stately way, had taken her seat, and Peter had swerved into his, Mr. Prosser said, "Peter Forrester."

"Yes?" Peter rose, scrabbling through his book for the right place.

"Kindly tell the class the exact meaning of the words 'Tomorrow, and tomorrow, and tomorrow/Creeps in this petty pace from day to day.'"

Peter glanced down at the high-school edition of *Macbeth* lying open on his desk. One of the duller girls tittered expectantly from the back of the room. Peter was popular with the girls; girls that age had minds like moths.

"Peter. With your book shut. We have all memorized this passage for today. Remember?" The girl in the back of the room squealed in delight. Gloria laid her own book face-open on her desk, where Peter could see it.

Peter shut his book with a bang and stared into Gloria's. "Why," he said at last, "I think it means pretty much what it says."

"Which is?"

"Why, that tomorrow is something we often think about. It creeps into our conversation all the time. We couldn't make any plans without thinking about tomorrow."

"I see. Then you would say that Macbeth is here referring to the, the date-book aspect of life?"

Geoffrey Langer laughed, no doubt to please Mr. Prosser. For a moment, he *was* pleased. Then he realized he had been playing for laughs at a student's expense.

His paraphrase had made Peter's reading of the lines seem more ridiculous than it was. He began to retract. "I admit—"

But Peter was going on; redheads never know when to quit. "Macbeth means that if we quit worrying about tomorrow, and just lived for today, we could appreciate all the wonderful things that are going on under our noses."

Mark considered this a moment before he spoke. He would not be sarcastic. "Uh, without denying that there is truth in what you say, Peter, do you think it likely that Macbeth, in his situation, would be expressing such"—he couldn't help himself—"such sunny sentiments?"

Geoffrey laughed again. Peter's neck reddened; he studied the floor. Gloria glared at Mr. Prosser, the anger in her face clearly meant for him to see.

Mark hurried to undo his mistake. "Don't misunderstand me, please," he told Peter. "I don't have all the answers myself. But it seems to me the whole speech, down to 'Signifying nothing,' is saying that life is— well, a *fraud*. Nothing wonderful about it."

"Did Shakespeare really think that?" Geoffrey Langer asked, a nervous quickness pitching his voice high.

Mark read into Geoffrey's question his own adolescent premonitions of the terrible truth. The attempt he must make was plain. He told Peter he could sit down and looked through the window toward the steadying sky. The clouds were gaining intensity.

"There is," Mr. Prosser slowly began, "much darkness in Shakespeare's work, and no play is darker than 'Macbeth.' The atmosphere is poisonous, oppressive. One critic has said that in this play, humanity suffocates." This was too fancy.

"In the middle of his career, Shakespeare wrote plays about men like Hamlet and Othello and Macbeth— men who aren't allowed by their society, or bad luck, or some minor flaw in themselves, to become the great men they might have been. Even Shakespeare's comedies of this period deal with a world gone sour. It is as if he had seen through the bright, bold surface of his earlier comedies and histories and had looked upon something terrible. It frightened him, just as some day it may frighten some of you." In his determination to find the right words, he had been staring at Gloria, without meaning to. Embarrassed, she nodded, and, realizing what had happened, he smiled at her.

He tried to make his remarks gentler, even diffident. "But then I think Shakespeare sensed a redeeming truth. His last plays are serene and symbolical, as if he had pierced through the ugly facts and reached a realm where the facts are again beautiful. In this way, Shakespeare's total work is a more complete image of life than that of any other writer, except perhaps for Dante, an Italian poet who wrote several centuries earlier." He had been taken far from the Macbeth soliloquy. Other teachers had been happy to tell him how the kids made a game of getting him talking. He looked toward Geoffrey. The boy was doodling on his tablet, indifferent. Mr. Prosser concluded, "The last play Shakespeare wrote is an extraordinary poem called 'The Tempest.' Some of you may want to read it for your next book reports—the ones due May 10th. It's a short play."

The class had been taking a holiday. Barry Snyder was snicking BBs off the blackboard and glancing over at Brute Young to see if he noticed. "Once more, Barry," Mr. Prosser said, "and out you go." Barry blushed, and grinned to cover the blush, his eyeballs sliding toward Brute. The dull girl in the rear of the room was putting on lipstick. "Put that away, Alice," Mr. Prosser commanded. She giggled and obeyed. Sejak, the Polish boy who worked nights, was asleep at his desk, his cheek white with pressure against the varnished wood, his mouth sagging sidewise. Mr. Prosser had an impulse to let him sleep. But the impulse might not be true kindness, but just the self-congratulatory, kindly pose in which he sometimes discovered himself. Besides, one breach of discipline encouraged others. He strode down the aisle and shook Sejak awake. Then he turned his attention to the mumble growing at the front of the room.

Peter Forrester was whispering to Gloria, trying to make her laugh. The girl's face, though, was cool and solemn, as if a thought had been provoked in her head. Perhaps at least *she* had been listening to what Mr. Prosser had been saying. With a bracing sense of chivalrous intercession, Mark said, "Peter. I gather from this noise that you have something to add to your theories."

Peter responded courteously. "No, sir. I honestly

don't understand the speech. Please, sir, what *does* it mean?"

This candid admission and odd request stunned the class. Every white, round face, eager, for once, to learn, turned toward Mark. He said, "I don't know. I was hoping *you* would tell *me*."

In college, when a professor made such a remark, it was with grand effect. The professor's humility, the necessity for creative interplay between teacher and student were dramatically impressed upon the group. But to 11D, ignorance in an instructor was as wrong as a hole in a roof. It was as if he had held forty strings pulling forty faces taut toward him and then had slashed the strings. Heads waggled, eyes dropped, voices buzzed. Some of the discipline problems, like Peter Forrester, smirked signals to one another.

"Quiet!" Mr. Prosser shouted. "All of you. Poetry isn't arithmetic. There's no single right answer. I don't want to force my own impression on you, even if I *have* had much more experience with literature." He made this last clause very loud and distinct, and some of the weaker students seemed reassured. "I know none of *you* want that," he told them.

Whether or not they believed him, they subsided, somewhat. Mark judged he could safely reassume his human-among-humans attitude again. He perched on the edge of the desk and leaned forward beseechingly. "Now, honestly. Don't any of you have some personal feeling about the lines that you would like to share with the class and me?"

One hand, with a flowered handkerchief balled in it,

: **33** :

unsteadily rose. "Go ahead, Teresa," Mr. Prosser said encouragingly. She was a timid, clumsy girl whose mother was a Jehovah's Witness.

"It makes me think of cloud shadows," Teresa said.

Geoffrey Langer laughed. "Don't be rude, Geoff," Mr. Prosser said sideways, softly, before throwing his voice forward: "Thank you, Teresa. I think that's an interesting and valid impression. Cloud movement has something in it of the slow, monotonous rhythm one feels in the line 'Tomorrow, and tomorrow, and tomorrow.' It's a very gray line, isn't it, class?" No one agreed or disagreed.

Beyond the windows actual clouds were bunching rapidly, and erratic sections of sunlight slid around the room. Gloria's arm, crooked gracefully above her head, turned gold. "Gloria?" Mr. Prosser asked.

She looked up from something on her desk with a face of sullen radiance. "I think what Teresa said was very good," she said, glaring in the direction of Geoffrey Langer. Geoffrey chuckled defiantly. "And I have a question. What does 'petty pace' mean?"

"It means the trivial day-to-day sort of life that, say, a bookkeeper or a bank clerk leads. Or a school-teacher," he added, smiling.

She did not smile back. Thought wrinkles irritated her perfect brow. "But Macbeth has been fighting wars, and killing kings, and being a king himself, and all," she pointed out.

"Yes, but it's just these acts Macbeth is condemning as 'nothing.' Can you see that?"

Gloria shook her head. "Another thing I worry about—isn't it silly for Macbeth to be talking to himself right in the middle of this war, with his wife just dead, and all?"

"I don't think so, Gloria. No matter how fast events happen, thought is faster."

His answer was weak; everyone knew it, even if Gloria hadn't mused, supposedly to herself, but in a voice the entire class could hear, "It seems so *stupid*."

Mark winced, pierced by the awful clarity with which his students saw him. Through their eyes, how queer he looked, with his long hands, and his horn-rimmed glasses, and his hair never slicked down, all wrapped up in "literature," where, when things get rough, the king mumbles a poem nobody understands. The delight Mr. Prosser took in such crazy junk made not only his good sense but his masculinity a matter of doubt. It was gentle of them not to laugh him out of the room. He looked down and rubbed his fingertips together, trying to erase the chalk dust. The class noise sifted into unnatural quiet. "It's getting late," he said finally. "Let's start the recitations of the memorized passage. Bernard Amilson, you begin."

Bernard had trouble enunciating, and his rendition began " 'T'mau 'n' t'mau 'n' t'mau.' " It was reassuring, the extent to which the class tried to repress its laughter. Mr. Prosser wrote "A" in his marking book opposite Bernard's name. He always gave Bernard A on recitations, despite the school nurse, who claimed there was nothing organically wrong with the boy's mouth.

It was the custom, cruel but traditional, to deliver recitations from the front of the room. Alice, when her turn came, was reduced to a helpless state by the first funny face Peter Forrester made at her. Mark let her hang up there a good minute while her face ripened to cherry redness, and at last forgave her. She may try it later. Many of the youngsters knew the passage gratifyingly well, though there was a tendency to leave out the line "To the last syllable of recorded time" and to turn "struts and frets" into "frets and struts" or simply "struts and struts." Even Sejak, who couldn't have looked at the passage before he came to class, got through it as far as "And then is heard no more."

Geoffrey Langer showed off, as he always did, by interrupting his own recitation with bright questions. "'Tomorrow, and tomorrow, and tomorrow,'" he said, "'creeps in'—shouldn't that be '*creep* in,' Mr. Prosser?"

"It is 'creep*s*.' The trio is in effect singular. Go on." Mr. Prosser was tired of coddling Langer. If you let them, these smart students will run away with the class. "Without the footnotes."

"'Creep*sss* in this petty pace from day to day, to the last syllable of recorded time, and all our yesterdays have lighted fools the way to dusty death. Out, out—'"

"No, no!" Mr. Prosser jumped out of his chair. "This is poetry. Don't mushmouth it! Pause a little after 'fools.'" Geoffrey looked genuinely startled this time, and Mark himself did not quite understand his annoyance and, mentally turning to see what was behind him, seemed to glimpse in the humid undergrowth the two stern eyes of the indignant look Gloria had thrown Geoffrey. He glimpsed himself in the absurd position of acting as Gloria's champion in her private war with this intelligent boy. He sighed apologetically. "Poetry is made up of lines," he began, turning to the class. Gloria was passing a note to Peter Forrester.

The rudeness of it! To pass notes during a scolding that she herself had caused! Mark caged in his hand the girl's frail wrist and ripped the note from her fingers. He read it to himself, letting the class see he was reading it, though he despised such methods of discipline. The note went:

> Pete— I think you're *wrong* about Mr. Prosser. I think he's wonderful and I get a lot out of his class. He's heavenly with poetry. I think I love him. I really do *love* him. So there.

Mr. Prosser folded the note once and slipped it into his side coat pocket. "See me after class, Gloria," he said. Then, to Geoffrey, "Let's try it again. Begin at the beginning."

While the boy was reciting the passage, the buzzer sounded the end of the period. It was the last class of the day. The room quickly emptied, except for Gloria. The noise of lockers slamming open and books being thrown against metal and shouts drifted in.

"Who has a car?"

"Lend me a cig, pig."

"We can't have practice in this slop."

Mark hadn't noticed exactly when the rain started, but it was coming down fast now. He moved around the room with the window pole, closing windows and pulling down shades. Spray bounced in on his hands. He began to talk to Gloria in a crisp voice that, like his device of shutting the windows, was intended to protect them both from embarrassment.

: 37 :

"About note passing." She sat motionless at her desk in the front of the room, her short, brushed-up hair like a cool torch. From the way she sat, her naked arms folded at her breasts and her shoulders hunched, he felt she was chilly. "It is not only rude to scribble when a teacher is talking, it is stupid to put one's words down on paper, where they look much more foolish than they might have sounded if spoken." He leaned the window pole in its corner and walked toward his desk.

"And about love. 'Love' is one of those words that illustrate what happens to an old, overworked language. These days, with movie stars and crooners and preachers and psychiatrists all pronouncing the word, it's come to mean nothing but a vague fondness for something. In this sense, I love the rain, this blackboard, these desks, you. It means nothing, you see, whereas once the word signified a quite explicit thing —a desire to share all you own and are with someone else. It is time we coined a new word to mean that, and when you think up the word *you* want to use, I suggest that you be economical with it. Treat it as something you can spend only once—if not for your own sake, for the good of the language." He walked over to his own desk and dropped two pencils on it, as if to say, "That's all."

"I'm sorry," Gloria said.

Rather surprised, Mr. Prosser said, "Don't be."

"But you don't understand."

"Of course I don't. I probably never did. At your age, I was like Geoffrey Langer."

"I bet you weren't." The girl was almost crying; he was sure of that.

"Come on, Gloria. Run along. Forget it." She slowly cradled her books between her bare arm and her sweater, and left the room with that melancholy shuffling teen-age gait, so that her body above her thighs seemed to float over the desks.

What was it, Mark asked himself, these kids were after? What did they want? Glide, he decided, the quality of glide. To slip along, always in rhythm, always cool, the little wheels humming under you, going nowhere special. If Heaven existed, that's the way it would be there. "He's heavenly with poetry." They loved the word. Heaven was in half their songs.

"Christ, he's humming." Strunk, the physical ed teacher, had come into the room without Mark's noticing. Gloria had left the door ajar.

"Ah," Mark said, "a fallen angel, full of grit."

"What the hell makes you so happy?"

"I'm not happy, I'm just serene. I don't know why you don't appreciate me."

"Say." Strunk came up an aisle with a disagreeably effeminate waddle, pregnant with gossip. "Did you hear about Murchison?"

"No." Mark mimicked Strunk's whisper.

"He got the pants kidded off him today."

"Oh dear."

Strunk started to laugh, as he always did before beginning a story. "You know what a goddam lady's man he thinks he is?"

"You bet," Mark said, although Strunk said that about every male member of the faculty.

"You have Gloria Angstrom, don't you?"

"You bet."

"Well, this morning Murky intercepts a note she was writing, and the note says what a damn neat guy she thinks Murchison is and how she *loves* him!" Strunk waited for Mark to say something, and then, when he didn't, continued, "You could see he was tickled pink. But—get this—it turns out at lunch that the same damn thing happened to Fryeburg in history yesterday!" Strunk laughed and cracked his knuckles viciously. "The girl's too dumb to have thought it up herself. We all think it was Peter Forrester's idea."

"Probably was," Mark agreed. Strunk followed him out to his locker, describing Murchison's expression when Fryeburg (in all innocence, mind you) told what had happened to him.

Mark turned the combination of his locker, 18–24–3. "Would you excuse me, Dave?" he said. "My wife's in town waiting."

Strunk was too thick to catch Mark's anger. "I got to get over to the gym. Can't take the little darlings outside in the rain; their mommies'll write notes to teacher." He clattered down the hall and wheeled at the far end, shouting, "Now don't tell You-know-who!"

Mr. Prosser took his coat from the locker and shrugged it on. He placed his hat upon his head. He fitted his rubbers over his shoes, pinching his fingers painfully, and lifted his umbrella off the hook. He thought of opening it right there in the vacant hall, as a kind of joke, and decided not to. The girl had been almost crying; he was sure of that.

Dentistry and Doubt

BURTON KNEW WHAT THE DENTIST WOULD NOTICE FIRST: the clerical collar. People always did. The dentist was standing not quite facing the door, as if it had just occurred to him to turn away. His eyes, gray in a rose, faintly mustached face, clung to Burton's throat a moment too long for complete courtesy before lifting as he said, "Hello!" Shifting his feet, the dentist thrust out an unexpectedly soft hand.

He noticed next that Burton was an American. In Oxford Burton had acquired the habit of speaking softly, but susurration alone could not alter the proportionate emphasis of vowel over consonant, the slight drag at the end of each sentence, or any of the diphthongal peculiarities that betray Americans to the twittering English. As soon as Burton had returned the greeting, with an apology for being late (he did not blame the British buses, though they were at fault), he fancied he could hear the other man's mind register:

"U.S.A. . . . pioneer piety . . . R.C.? Can't be; no black hat . . . frank enough smile . . . rather heavy tartar on the incisors."

He motioned Burton to the chair and turned to a sink, where he washed his hands without looking at them. He talked over his shoulder. "What part are you from?"

"Of the States?" Burton enjoyed saying "the States." It sounded so aggregate, so ominous.

"Yes. Are you Canadian?"

"No, I'm from Pennsylvania." Burton had never had such a good view from a dentist's chair. A great bay window gave on a small back yard. Black shapes of birds fluttered and jiggled among the twigs of two or three trees—willows, he guessed. Except for the birds, the trees were naked. A wet-wash sky hung, it seemed, a few feet behind the net of limbs. A brick wall looked the shade of rust, and patches of sky hinted at blue, but there was little color in any of it.

"Pennsylvania," the dentist mused, the latter syllables of the word amplifying as he drew closer. "That's in the East?"

"It's a Middle Atlantic state. You know where New York City is?"

"Roughly."

"It's a little west of that, more or less. It's a neutral sort of state."

"I see." The dentist leaned over him, and Burton received two wonderful surprises: when he opened his mouth the dentist said "Thank you"; and the dentist had something on his breath that, without being either, smelled sweet as candy and spicy as cloves. Peering in, he bumped a mirror across Burton's teeth. An electric reflector like an eye doctor's was strapped to his head. Outside, the big black birds did stunts among the twigs. The dentist's eyes were not actually gray; screwed up, they seemed more brown, and then, as they flicked toward the tool tray, rather green, like pebbles on the bed of a fast-running creek. He scraped at an eyetooth, but with such tact that Burton felt nothing. "There's certainly one," he said, turning to make a mark on a clean card.

Burton took the opportunity to rid himself of a remark he had been holding in suspension. "More than ninety per cent of the world's anthracite comes from Pennsylvania."

"Really?" the dentist said, obviously not believing him. He returned his hands, the tools in them, to in front of Burton's chin. Burton opened his mouth. "Thank you," the dentist said.

As he peered and picked and made notations, a measure of serenity returned to Burton. That morning, possibly because of the scheduled visit to a foreign dentist, the Devil had been very active. Skepticism had mingled with the heat and aroma of his bed; it had dripped from the cold ochre walls of his digs; it had been the substance of his dreams. His slippers, his bathrobe, his face in the mirror, his books—black books, brown ones, C. S. Lewis, Karl Barth, *The Portable Medieval Reader*, Raymond Tully and Bertrand Russell lying together as nonchalantly as if they had been Belloc and Chesterton—stood witness to a futility that undercut all hope and theory. Even his toothbrush, which on good days presented itself as an acolyte of matinal devotion, today seemed an agent of atheistic hygiene, broadcasting the hideous fact of germs. The faucet's merry gurgle had sounded over Burton's sudden prayers.

The scent of candy and cloves lifted. The dentist, standing erect, was asking, "Do you take novocain?"

Burton hesitated. He believed that one of the lazier modern assumptions was the identification of pain with evil. Indeed, insofar as pain warned us of corruption, it was good. On the other hand, relieving the pain of others was an obvious virtue—perhaps the *most* obvious virtue. And to court pain was as morbid as to chase pleasure. Yet to flee from pain was clearly cowardice.

The dentist, not hinting by his voice whether he had been waiting for an answer several seconds or no time at all, asked, "Does your dentist at home give you novocain?"

Ever since Burton was a little boy in crusty dungarees, Dr. Gribling had given him novocain. "Yes." The answer sounded abrupt, impolite. Burton added, "He says my nerves are exceptionally large." It was a pompous thing to say.

"We'll do the eyetooth," the dentist said.

Burton's heart beat like a wasp in a jar as the dentist moved across the room, did unseeable things by the sink, and returned with a full hypodermic. A drop of fluid, by some miracle of adhesion, clung trembling to the needle's tip. Burton opened his mouth while the dentist's back was still turned. When at last the man pivoted, his instrument tilting up, a tension beneath his mustache indicated surprise and perhaps amusement at finding things in such readiness. "Open a little wider, please," he said. "Thank you." The needle moved closer. It was under Burton's nose and out of focus. "Now, this might hurt a little." What a kind thing to say! The sharp prick and the consequent slow, filling ache drove Burton's eyes up, and he saw the tops of the bare willow trees, the frightened white sky, and the black birds. As he watched, one bird joined another on the topmost twig, and then a third joined these two and the twig became radically cresent, and all three birds flapped off to where his eyes could not follow them.

"There," the dentist sighed, in a zephyr of candy and cloves.

Waiting for the novocain to take effect, Burton and the dentist made conversation.

"And what brings you to Oxford?" the dentist began.

"I'm doing graduate work."

"Oh? What sort?"

"I'm doing a thesis on a man called Richard Hooker."

"Oh?" The dentist sounded as incredulous as he had about Pennsylvania's anthracite.

Richard Hooker—"pious, peaceable, primitive," in Walton's phrase—loomed so large in Burton's world that to doubt Hooker's existence was in effect to doubt the existence of Burton's world. But he added the explanatory "An English divine" without the least bit of irritability or condescension. The lesson of humility was one that had come rather easily to Burton. He recognized, however, that in his very thinking of his own humility he was guilty of pride, and his immediate rec-

ognition of it as pride was foundation for further, sub-
tler egotism.

He would have harried the sin to its source had not
the dentist said, "A divine is a church writer?"

"That's right."

"Could you quote me something he wrote?"

Burton had expected, and was prepared to answer,
several questions ("When did he live?" "1554 to 1600."
"What is the man's claim to fame?" "He attempted to
reconcile Christian—that is, Thomist—political theory
with the actual state of things under the Tudor mon-
archy; he didn't really succeed, but he did anticipate
much of modern political thought." "What is your
thesis?" "Mostly an attempt to get at reasons for
Hooker's failure to come to grips with Renaissance
Platonism"), but he was unprepared for this one.
Scraps and phrases—"visible Church," "law eternal,"
"very slender ability," "Popish superstition," the odd
word "scrupulosity"—came to mind, but no rounded
utterance formed itself. "I can't think of anything
right now," he apologized, touching his fingers to his
collar and, as still sometimes happened, being taken
aback by the hard, unbroken edge they met.

The dentist did not seem disappointed. "Feel numb
yet?" he asked.

Burton tested and said, "Yes."

The dentist swung the drilling apparatus into place
and Burton opened his mouth. "Thank you." The
novocain had taken. The drilling at the tooth seemed
vastly distant, and it hurt no more than the explosion of
a star, or the death of an elephant in India, or, Burton

realized, the whipping of a child right next door. Pain. The problem presented itself. He slipped into the familiar arguments he used with himself. Creation is His seeking to make souls out of matter. Morally, matter, per se, is neutral—with form imposed upon it, good, but in any case its basic nature is competitive. No two things can occupy the same place at the same time. Hence, pain. But we must act with non-material motives. What was His journey on earth but a flouting of competitive values? And then there is the Devil. But with the Devil the whole cosmos became confused, and Burton's attention, by default, rested on the black birds. They kept falling out of the sky and the treetops, but he noticed few ascending.

The dentist changed his drill. "Thank you." There were things Burton could comprehend. And then there were things he could not—His aeon-long wait as life struggled up from the atom. With what emotion did He watch all those preposterous, earnest beasts labor up out of the swamp and aimlessly perish on the long and crooked road to Man? And the stars, so far off, the comedy of waste spaces—theologians had always said infinite, but could they have meant *that* infinite? Once, Burton had asked his father if he believed in purgatory. "Of course I do," he had snapped, jabbing toward the floor with his pipestem. "*This* is purgatory." Remembering the incident so depressed Burton that when the drill broke through the shell of anesthetic and bit his nerve, it came in the shape of an answer, and he greeted the pain with something like ecstacy.

"There," the dentist said. "Would you care to wash

out, please." He swung the drilling apparatus over to one side, so Burton could see it wouldn't be used any more. He was so kind.

"There seems to be a lot of birds in your back yard," Burton said to him.

"We have a feeding station," the dentist said, grinding the silver for the filling in a thick glass cup.

"What are those black birds?"

"Starlings. A greedy bird. They take everything they can away from the wren."

For the first time, Burton noticed some smaller shapes among the branches, quicker, but less numerous and less purposeful than the black birds. He watched one in particular, swivelling on his perch, now a formless blob, like a big bud, the next moment in vivid profile, like a Picasso ceramic. As he watched the bird, his mind emptied itself, and nothing, not even the squeaking of the silver, disturbed it.

When he again became conscious, it was of the objects on the tray before him as things in which an unlimited excitement inhered; the tweezers, the picks, the drill burrs, the celluloid container of cotton, the tiny cotton balls, the metal cup where a flame could burn, the enamelled construction beside him housing a hundred useful devices, the tiled walls, the window frame, the things beyond the window—all travelled to his senses burdened with delight and power. The sensation was one that Burton had frequently enjoyed in his childhood and more and more rarely as he aged. His urge to laugh, or to *do* something with the objects, was repressed, and even the smile he gave the dentist was lost, for the man was concerned with keeping a dab of silver on the end of a golf-club-shaped tool.

Burton received the silver. He thought of the world as being, like all music, founded on tension. The tree pushing up, gravity pulling down, the bird desiring to fill the air, the air compelled to crush the bird. His head brimmed with irrelevant recollections: a rubber Donald Duck he had owned, and abused, as an infant; the grape arbor in his parents' back yard; the respect his father commanded throughout his town; Shibe Park in sunlight; Max Beerbohm's sentence about there always being a slight shock in seeing an envelope of one's own after it has gone through the post.

The dentist coughed. It was the sound not of a man who has to cough but of one who has done his job, and can cough if he pleases. "Would you like to wash out, please?" He gestured toward a glass filled with pink fluid, which up to this time Burton had ignored. Burton took some of the liquid into his mouth (it was good, but not as good as the dentist's breath), sloshed it around, and, as silently as possible, spat it into the impeccable basin. "I'm afraid three or four trips are called for," the dentist said, studying his card.

"Fine."

The dentist's mustache stretched fractionally. "Miss Leviston will give you the appointments." One by one, he dropped the drill burrs into a compartmented drawer. "Do you have any idea why your teeth should be so, ah, indifferent?"

Burton concentrated. He yearned to thank the man, to bless him even, but since there was no conventional way to do that, he would show his gratitude by giving everything the dentist said his closest attention. "I believe Pennsylvania has one of the worst dental records of any state."

"Really? And why should that be?"

"I don't know. I think the Southern states have the best teeth. They eat fish, or turnip tops, or something with lots of calcium in it."

"I see." The dentist moved aside so Burton could climb out of the chair. "Until next time, then."

Burton supposed they would not shake hands twice in one visit. Near the doorway, he turned. "Oh, Doctor, uh . . ."

"Merritt," the dentist said.

"I just thought of a quotation from Hooker. It's just a short sentence."

"Yes?"

" 'I grant we are apt, prone, and ready, to forsake God; but is God as ready to forsake us? Our minds are changeable; is His so likewise?' "

Dr. Merritt smiled. The two men stood in the same position they had hesitated in when Burton entered the room. Burton smiled. Outside the window, the wrens and the starlings, mixed indistinguishably, engaged in maneuvers that seemed essentially playful.

The Kid's Whistling

THINGS WERE NEARLY PERFECT: CHRISTMAS WAS THREE weeks away, Roy worked late every evening and was doubling his salary in overtime, and tonight rain was falling. Rain was Roy's favorite sensation, and he never felt more at rest, more at home, than when working nights in his hot little room on the third floor of Herlihy's—the department store stretching dark and empty under him, the radio murmuring, maybe the rain tapping on the black skylight, the engines shuttling back and forth in the Buchanan Street freight yards, a mile away.

The one trouble was the kid's whistling. For ten months a year Roy had the Display Department to himself. If the orders for counter cards piled up, Shipping lent him a boy to help out. But at the beginning of November, Simmons, the store manager, hired a high-school kid to come in weekday evenings and on Saturdays. This year's helper was called Jack, and he whistled. He whistled all the time.

At the hand press, Jack was printing counter cards and rendering "Summertime." He seemed to feel the tune needed a cool, restrained treatment, for which Roy was grateful; he was all set to begin the Toy Department sign and wanted things to go well. Though the customary sans-serif or bold roman would have done, he planned to try Old English capitals. It was for his own satisfaction; no one would appreciate the extra effort, least of all Simmons. On a plywood board, ½″ x 1½′ x 11′, primed with off-white, Roy ruled the guidelines and pencilled the letters lightly, mostly to get the spacing. He lit a cigarette, puffed it a moment, not inhaling, then set it on the edge of the workbench. His drawing board was hinged to the second of four shelves; in working position, the board rested upon and overhung the rim of the bench at an angle of thirty degrees. When not in use, the board was supposed to hook into a loop screw attached to the top shelf, but the screw had worked out of the soft, cheap pine, and the board always hung down. This way, the lowest shelf was half concealed, and had become a cave of empty paint jars, forgotten memos, petrified brushes, scraps of Masonite. On the second shelf, in rainbow order, the jars of poster paints sat. The third shelf held jars of nails, boxes of tacks and staples, two staplers (one broken), colored inks (dried up), penholders in a wire loop, pen points in a cigar box, three hammers, two steel rods intended to brace the arms of mannequins, and a hand-jigsaw frame without a blade; these things were not as well ordered as the poster paints.

The tall space between the fourth shelf and the ceiling contained a blackened chaos of obsolete displays—silhouettes of Indians, firecrackers, reindeer, clouds, dollar-signs. Shelves in ascending degrees of muddle also covered the wall on Roy's left. To his right, at some distance, were the kid and the hand press and the entrance door. Behind him were the power tools, some timber, and the mannequin closet, built into the dimmest corner of the room. Though Roy had a long-legged stool, he stood at his drawing board. He chose a No. 9 wedge brush and a jar of Sky Blue poster paint. He glanced into the lettering book, open to "Old English." He made certain the shaker of Silverdust was within reach.

Then, with no more hesitation, Roy dipped the brush and touched it to the board. The great crescent of the T went on without a tremor. The broad curve capping it had just the proper jaunty hint of a left-to-right downslant. With a No. 2 brush he added the hairlines. He sprinkled Silverdust over the moist letter, blew the loose stuff away, and stepped back, pleased.

In his head Roy slammed a door shut on Jack's insistent version of "Lady Be Good." He shook his brush clean in a jar of water and executed the O in Deep Yellow. He was not sure that the yellow would stand out enough against the white, but it did, especially after the Silverdust was added.

Jack switched to "After You've Gone," doing it loud, tapping a foot. It got so trumpety that, in the middle of putting the hairline on the Y, Roy, afraid his hand might shake, turned and stared burningly at Jack's spine. It made no impression. Jack was tall, about six inches taller than Roy, and thin. His neck, no thicker than an arm, led into a muff of uncut hair. Clapping two pieces of type on the table, the kid leaned back and let fly four enormous, jubilant notes.

"Hey, Jack," Roy called.

The boy turned. "Beg pardon?" He looked startled, exposed. He wasn't one of these mean kids, actually.

"What about a Coke?"

"Suure. If you're having one."

Roy didn't want a soft drink; he wanted quiet. But he had worked himself into a position where there was nothing to do but go out into the dark hall, dig two dimes from his pocket, insert them in the machine, draw forth two wet bottles, and take them back to the Display Department. When he offered Jack one, the boy offered him a nickel and five pennies. "Keep it," Roy told him. "Buy yourself a saxophone."

Jack's grateful face showed that the hint had been too subtle for him. "Have some peanuts?" he said, gesturing toward an ink-smudged bag stamped PLANTERS.

The cold weight of the bottle in Roy's fingers made salted nuts seem appropriate. He took a good handful, then, noticing the bag was nearly empty, dropped some back into it. As he fed them to himself, one by one, the kid watched, apparently expecting conversation. Roy pointed with a loosely clenched hand at the sheaf of orders on the spindle. "Good night's work there."

"I can't get all them out tonight."

Roy knew this was so, but if he agreed, it might encourage the kid to loaf. He returned to his sign without another word. He polished off the fine lines of the

Y and, in one slow, satisfying movement of his arm, did the tail.

Washing both brushes, opening the jar labelled "Crimson," Roy was conscious of his hands. They were square and smooth, with dandified nails, and completely clean, yet not so white that they could not take a flattering tan from the contrast with the brilliant cuffs. The cuffs, folded back exactly twice and starched to about the stiffness of thin cardboard, pressed lightly on the flats of his forearms and gave him an agreeable packaged feeling. It was just as well he hadn't bawled the kid out. Roy knew it was only the boy's kind of peace, standing over there whistling, playing with type, his crusty apron snug around him, his bag of salted peanuts and his pack of Old Golds beside him on the table, God knows what going on in his brain. The kid smoked steadily. Once, when Roy asked Jack if he didn't smoke too much, Jack had said no, this was the only place he ever smoked, which was exactly the point, but Roy let it drop. It wasn't as if he was the kid's father.

Roy started the L. Jack started "If I Could Be With You One Hour Tonight," in an irritating, loose, whoopsy way. Trying to be Coleman Hawkins or some bop son of a bitch. Hoping to get something across, Roy switched on the radio he kept on the shelf. It was an old Philco; its tubes were all but shot. Even on full, it wasn't loud enough for Jack to hear above his own noise. He kept on whistling, like this was Heaven.

Roy finished up the L. Suddenly Jack went quiet. Roy, hoping the kid wasn't offended, turned off his radio. In the silence, he heard the sounds that had really made the kid stop: the elevator door clanging shut and then heels clicking.

More than a minute seemed to pass before the Display Department door opened. When it did, there was Janet, wearing a transparent raincoat, moisture beaded all over it and in her clipped red hair. There was something aggressive about that soaked hair. She frowned in the brilliant light. "It's dark out there," she said. "I got lost."

"The switch is right by the elevator" was all Roy could think of to say.

Janet walked past the printing machine, with the kid at it, and came to stand by Roy. She looked at the sign. " 'Todl?' " she read.

" 'Toyl.' That's a Y."

"But it's closed at the top. It looks like a D with a wiggly tail."

"This is Gothic lettering."

"Well, I don't want to argue. It's probably just me."

"How come you're down here? What's up?"

"The rain made me restless."

"You walked all the way? Who let you into the store?"

"It's only six blocks. I don't mind walking in the rain. I like it." Janet's head was tilted and her hands were busy at an earring. "The watchman let me in. He said, 'You go right on up, Mrs. Mays. He'll be glad to see you. He'll be real lonely and happy to see you.' "

"Orley let you in?"

"I didn't ask his name." She took a cigarette from Roy's pack.

"Better take off your raincoat," Roy said. "You don't want to catch cold."

She shrugged it off, draped it over the electric jigsaw, and stood, her legs spread as far as her narrow skirt allowed, smoking and studying the stuff in the top rack. Roy drew down the Orange and began painting the A.

"Orange next to red," she said. "Ooey."

"Hih," he grunted, not hard enough to jiggle his hand.

"What's in these boxes?"

"Boxes?" Roy was concentrating and barely heard what she said.

"*These* boxes."

He lifted the brush and looked around to see what she was pointing at. "Tinsel."

"Tinsel! Why, you have two, four, six, *six* huge crates of it here! What do you *do* with it all? Sleep in it? Do you feed it to cows?"

"You get a reduction for quantity."

She kicked one of the crates thoughtfully and moved on, inspecting. The last time Janet had come into Herlihy's was over three months ago, to pick him up for dinner and a movie. She hadn't been in this mood then. "Why don't you clean this mess out?" she called in a resonant, boxed-in voice from the closet where the mannequins were stored.

"Be careful. Those things cost." Roy pointed up the big sweeping serif on the A.

She came back into the room. "What are these for?"

He doused the wet letter with Silverdust before

turning to see what she meant. "They're pine boughs."

"I know *that*. I mean what are you going to *do* with them?"

"What do you mean, what am I going to do with them? Put them in the window, make wreaths. This is Christmas, for Chrissake."

He turned his back on her and stared at his sign. She came over and stood beside him. He began the N. As he completed the downstroke, his elbow touched her side, she was standing that close.

"When are you coming home?" she asked softly, for the first time acting like there was a third person in the room.

"What time is it now?"

"A little after nine."

"I don't see how I can get away before eleven. I have to finish this sign."

"It's almost done now."

"I have to finish the sign; then I thought the kid and I would hang it up. And then there are other things to do. It piles up. I'll try to make it by eleven—"

"Roy, *really*."

"I'll try to make it by eleven, but I can't guarantee it. I'm *sorry*, honey, but Simmons is on my neck all the time. What the hell: I'm getting time and a half."

She was silent while he put the serifs on the N. "So I suppose there's no point in my waiting around here," she said at last.

The N looked fine. In fact, the entire sign was more than passable. He was rather proud of himself, that he hadn't let her rattle him.

"I'll see you around eleven," Janet said. She was putting on her raincoat.

"Here, let me walk you out."

"Oh, no." She lifted a long pale sarcastic palm. "Don't let *me* disturb you. Time and a half, you know. I can flounder out on my own."

Roy decided, seeing the mood she was in, that it would be better to let her make whatever point she thought she was making.

By way of patching things up, he watched her leaving. He could tell from the cocky, hollow-backed way she walked toward the door that she knew his eyes were on her. Instead of passing by Jack's bench, she paused and said, "Hello. What keeps *you* up so late?"

Jack rolled his eyes toward the racks of freshly inked signs. "Printing these."

"All those on this little thing?" Janet touched the press. "Inky!"

She showed Jack the first and second fingers of her hand; each was tipped with a crimson spot the size of a confetti bit. The kid poked around helplessly for a clean rag. The best he could do was offer her a corner of his apron. "Thank you so much." She wiped her fingers slowly, thoroughly. At the door, she smiled and said "Goodbye, all," to a point in the room midway between her husband and the boy.

Roy chose to paint the last letter, D, in Sky Blue again, the same as the initial T. It would give the thing unity. As he formed the letter, first with the No. 9 brush, then with the No. 2, he was aware of something out of place, something askew, in his room, and with a section of his mind he tried to locate the trouble. This was a mistake. When the letter was covered with Silverdust, Roy stepped back and saw that he had botched it. The D was too plump, out of scale, too close to the N. It was nothing Simmons or anybody would notice—who looked at signs, anyway?—but Roy knew it had been ruined, and now knew why. The kid had stopped whistling.

Toward Evening

Waiting for a number five bus in front of St. Patrick's Cathedral, Rafe was tired and hence dreamy. When the bus at last came and a short fatty woman in black bounced in front of him and then stopped, apparently paralyzed, right at the open doors, with the bus driver tapping the wheel and Rockefeller's towers gathered above them like a thunderhead, Rafe was not very much surprised. The woman made metallic, agitated noises. She seemed unable to step up, to grab the vertical bar, to move away, to do anything. Her hat, black straw strewn with purple berries, quivered, whether with indignation or fright, there was no telling. "Here we go," Rafe said, grabbing her a few inches below the armpits and hoisting. The woman was filled with sand. The only thing that worried Rafe was, he was carrying in one hand, by a loop of string, a box containing a mobile for the baby and didn't want it crushed.

"Oh, thank you!" a chirping voice beneath the hat cried even before she was safe on the step. "Thank you so much, whoever you are." His face seemed to be in her hat; he could see little else. The cloth beneath his fingers turned moist and kept slipping; Rafe had the hideous notion that something would break, and the sack spill, and the woman angrily sink to the pavement as a head in a nest of vacant clothing, like Ray Bolger in *The Wizard of Oz*. Suddenly, when her ascension seemed impossible, she was up, and his freed hands jerked, as if birds had flown from them.

"Wasn't that kind?" the woman asked the bus driver, not turning, though, and never showing Rafe her face.

"Move to the rear," the driver said in the soft level tones of the poor disciplinarian. Holding the box close to his chest, Rafe edged through the bodies, hunting a porcelain loop. The woman in black had disappeared, yet she couldn't have found a seat. And in the rear of the bus, where there was ample standing space, a beautiful girl stood. Two ash-blue streaks had been symmetrically dyed into her oloroso-colored hair. Her topcoat, box-style and black, hung open, half-sheathing her body. Her feet, in gray heels, were planted on the sides of an invisible V. Numberless Vs were visible wherever two edges of the pencil-stripe fabric of her suit met: in a straight seam down her back, along her sleeves, within her lapels, at the side of her skirt (very acute, these). At the base of her throat, where a V seemed promised, something more complex occurred, involving the sheathed extremities of opposed collarbones, the tapered shelves of their upper edges, the two nervous and rather thoroughbred cords of her neck, and between them a hollow where you could lay a tea-spoon. She was less tall than her thinness made her appear; her forehead was level with Rafe's chin.

The bus veered. The standees swung, and her face, until then averted, turned toward his, a fine face, lucid brow. The kind of mouth you felt spoke French. If her nose had been smaller it would have been too small. The indentation in the center of the upper lip—the romantic dimple, Rafe's mother had called it, claiming, in the joking, sentimental way she had assumed to raise a child, that in its depth the extent of sexual vigor could be read—was narrow and incisive. Rafe was wondering about her eyes when she turned them up from her book to stare at him for staring, and he lowered his lids too quickly to gain any prize but a meagre impression of bigness. The book in her hand was *A l'ombre des jeunes filles en fleurs.*

After a few moments, he felt that even studying her hand was an intrusion in the ellipse of repose focused on the twin points of face and book. Rafe hugged the box containing the mobile and, stooping down, looked out of the bus window. They had rounded Columbus Circle and were headed up Broadway. The clearly marked numbers on the east side of the street ran: 1832, 1836, 1846, 1850 (Wordsworth dies), 1880 (great Nihilist trial in St. Petersburg), 1900 (Rafe's father born in Trenton), 1902 (Braque leaves Le Havre to study painting in Paris), 1914 (Joyce begins *Ulysses;* war begins in Europe), 1926 (Rafe's parents marry in Ithaca), 1936 (Rafe is four years old). Where the present should have stood, a block was torn down, and the numbering began again with 2000, a boring progressive edifice. Rafe diverted his attention from the window to the poster above it. The poster ingeniously advertised Jomar Instant Coffee. The gimmick was a finely corrugated cellulose sheet in which had been embedded two positions of a depicted man's eyeball, arm, and lips. Ideally, from one angle the man was seen holding a cup of coffee to his mouth, smiling, and in flavorful ecstasy rolling his iris to the top of his egg-shaped eye; from another angle he appeared with the cup lowered, his eyeball also lowered, and his lips parted in downright laughter. Rafe's closeness and the curvature of the bus roof prevented the illusion from working with complete success. Both arms, both eyeballs, were always present, though with seesaw intensity as Rafe ducked his head up and down. Either the Jomar man's openmouthed grin was intersected by the ghost of his closedmouthed smile; or the latter was surrounded by the shadow of the former. Rafe began to feel bus-sick.

He returned to the girl. She was there, beside him, but leaving. Proust jutted from her pocketbook. Her face wore the enamelled look of a person who has emerged from a piece of fiction into the world of decisions. With a whispering touch, her backside eased past his. Having pulled the green cord, she waited in front of the side doors, her profile a brilliant assault on the atmosphere. The doors flapped open. Pursing her mouth, she managed the step, walked south, and was gone.

The entry of some new passengers forced Rafe deeper into the rear of the bus, yards away from where

he had stood with the girl. Bit by bit, in confused order, as word of a disaster first filters in over the wires,
he became conscious of the young Negress seated beneath him. Her baby-flat nose was a good glossy place
for his attention to rest. When she recrossed her legs,
he noticed the unpatterned breadth of turquoise skirt,
the yellow coat clashing with it, the tense hair painfully pulled straight, the hard-to-read foreshortened
curves of her face, the hands folded, with an odd precision, in her turquoise lap. She was wearing blue half-
gloves; they stopped at the base of her thumbs. It was
the hint of grotesqueness needed to make Rafe lustful.
Yet the girl, in becoming desirable, became inacces-
sible. If Rafe looked at her more steadily than at his
previous love, it was because the distance her power
established rendered her tactually insensitive to long
looks. Likewise, because his imaginings concerning
himself and the girl were so plainly fantastic, he could
indulge them without limit.

The pure life of the mind, for all its quick distances,
is soon tedious. Rafe, dwelling again on the actual
Negress, observed the prim secretarial carriage of her
head, the orange skin, the sarcastic Caucasian set of
her lips. Dress women in sea and sand or pencil lines,
they were chapters on the same subject, no more unlike than St. Paul and Paul Tillich. In the end, when he
alighted at Eighty-fifth Street, the Negress had dwindled to the thought that he had never seen gloves like
that before.

Behind him the bus doors closed: pterodactyl wings.
A woman standing on the deserted pavement stared at
the long box, never guessing a mobile for a baby was

in it. The warm air, moistened by the Hudson, guaranteed Spring. Rafe went up the rounded, coral-colored steps, across the checkered lobby floor, and into the tiny scarlet elevator, which was nearly always waiting for him, like a loyal but not slavish dog. Inside his apartment, the baby had just been fed and was laughing; her mother, flushed and sleepy, lay in a slip on the sofa bed.

That invisible gas, goodness, stung his eyes and made him laugh, strut, talk nonsense. He held the baby at arm's height, lowered her until her belly rested on the top of his head, and walked rapidly around the room singing, "I have a little babe, her name is Liz, I think she's better than she really is, I think she's better than she ever will be, what ev-er will, become of me?"

The baby laughed, "Gkk, ngk!"

The mobile was not a success. Alice had expected a genuine Calder, made of beautiful polished woods, instead of seven rubber birds with celluloid wings, hung from a piece of coarse wire. Elizabeth wanted to put the birds in her mouth and showed no interest in, perhaps did not even see, their abstract swinging, quite unlike the rapt infant shown on the box.

The baby went to sleep and Alice prepared the dinner in an atmosphere of let-down.

"I saw some funny gloves today," Rafe called. There was no answer from the kitchen, just the sound of pans.

When dinner came, it was his favorite everything—peas, hamburger, baked potato, cooked to avoid his allergies, served on the eccentric tilting plates in which, newly married, and they had sailed the clean seas of sophistication.

It was growing dark, spottily. A curious illusion was unexpectedly created: his wife, irritated because he had failed to answer some question of hers—her questions about his life at the office, so well meant, so understandable in view of her own confined existence, numbed his mind to the extent that not only his recent doings but her questions themselves were obliterated —dropped a triangular piece of bread from her fingers, and the bread, falling to her lap through a width of light, twirled and made a star.

From where he sat, dinner done, smoking a cigarette, Rafe could look across the Hudson to the Palisades, surmounted by seeming villages. A purple sky was being lowered over a yellow one. The Spry sign went on. The sign, which by virtue of brightness and readability dominated their night view, had three stages: Spry (red), Spry (white) FOR BAKING (red), and Spry (white) FOR FRYING (red). Rafe sometimes wondered how it had come to be there. Some executive, no doubt, had noticed the bare roof of the newly acquired waterfront plant. "We could use a Spry sign there," he murmured to his secretary, whom he had kept late at the office and was driving to her home in Riverdale. The following Monday, the secretary made an interdepartmental memo of J.G.'s remark. The man second in charge of Public Relations (the man first in charge was on vacation in the Poconos), new at the job, seven years out of Yale, and not bold enough to take J.G. with a grain of salt, told a man in the Creative End to draw up a sketch. After three days, the man in Creative did this, basing his sketch upon a hundred-and-eighty-six-pound file of past Spry ads. The man in Public Relations had a boy take it into the head office. J.G., flattered to have his suggestion followed up, wrote on the back, "Turn it slightly south. Nobody at Columbia cooks," and passed it on, OKed. The two other executives who saw the sketch (both of whom, by an almost supernatural coincidence, had daughters at Sarah Lawrence threatening marriage) suspected that J.G. was developing power among the stockholders and shrewdly strung along. Bids were requested and submitted. One was accepted. The neon people shaped the tubes. Metalworkers constructed a frame. On a November Tuesday, the kind of blowy day that gives you earache, the sign was set in place by eighteen men, the youngest of whom would someday be an internationally known stage actor. At 3:30, an hour and a half before they were supposed to quit, they knocked off and dispersed, because the goddam job was done. Thus the Spry sign (thus the river, thus trees, thus babies and sleep) came to be.

Above its winking, the small cities had disappeared. The black of the river was as wide as that of the sky. Reflections sunk in it existed dimly, minutely wrinkled, below the surface. The Spry sign occupied the night with no company beyond the also uncreated but illegible stars.

Snowing
in Greenwich Village

THE MAPLES HAD MOVED JUST THE DAY BEFORE TO WEST
Thirteenth Street, and that evening they had Rebecca
Cune over, because now they were so close. A tall, always slightly smiling girl with an absent manner, she
allowed Richard Maple to slip off her coat and scarf
even as she stood gently greeting Joan. Richard, moving with an extra precision and grace because of the
smoothness with which the business had been managed—though he and Joan had been married nearly
two years, he was still so young-looking that people
did not instinctively lay upon him hostly duties; their
reluctance worked in him a corresponding hesitancy,
so that often it was his wife who poured the drinks,
while he sprawled on the sofa in the attitude of a
favored and wholly delightful guest—entered the dark

: 69 :

bedroom, entrusted the bed with Rebecca's clothes, and returned to the living room. Her coat had seemed weightless.

Rebecca, seated beneath the lamp, on the floor, one leg tucked under her, one arm up on the Hide-a-Bed that the previous tenants had not as yet removed, was saying, "I had known her, you know, just for the day she taught me the job, but I said okay. I was living in an awful place called a hotel for ladies. In the halls they had typewriters you put a quarter in."

Joan, straightbacked on a Hitchcock chair from her parents' home in Vermont, a damp handkerchief balled in her hand, turned to Richard and explained, "Before her apartment now, Becky lived with this girl and her boy friend."

"Yes, his name was Jacques," Rebecca said.

Richard asked, "You lived with them?" The arch composure of his tone was left over from the mood aroused in him by his successful and, in the dim bedroom, somewhat poignant—as if he were with great tact delivering a disappointing message—disposal of their guest's coat.

"Yes, and he insisted on having his name on the mailbox. He was terribly afraid of missing a letter. When my brother was in the Navy and came to see me and saw on the mailbox"—with three parallel movements of her fingers she set the names beneath one another—

"Georgene Clyde,
Rebecca Cune,
Jacques Zimmerman,

he told me I had always been such a nice girl. Jacques wouldn't even move out so my brother would have a place to sleep. He had to sleep on the floor." She lowered her lids and looked in her purse for a cigarette.

"Isn't that wonderful?" Joan said, her smile broadening helplessly as she realized what an inane thing it had been to say. Her cold worried Richard. It had lasted seven days without improving. Her face was pale, mottled pink and yellow; this accentuated the Modiglianesque quality established by her long neck and oval blue eyes and her habit of sitting to her full height, her head quizzically tilted and her hands palm downward in her lap.

Rebecca, too, was pale, but in the consistent way of a drawing, perhaps—the weight of her lids and a certain virtuosity about the mouth suggested it—by da Vinci.

"Who would like some sherry?" Richard asked in a deep voice, from a standing position.

"We have some hard stuff if you'd rather," Joan said to Rebecca; from Richard's viewpoint the remark, like those advertisements which from varying angles read differently, contained the quite legible declaration that this time *he* would have to mix the Old Fashioneds.

"The sherry sounds fine," Rebecca said. She enunciated her words distinctly, but in a faint, thin voice that disclaimed for them any consequence.

"I think, too," Joan said.

"Good." Richard took from the mantel the eight-dollar bottle of Tio Pepe that the second man on the Spanish sherry account had stolen for him. So all could share in the drama of it, he uncorked the bottle in the living room. He posingly poured out three glasses, half-full, passed them around, and leaned against the mantel (the Maples had never had a mantel before), swirling the liquid, as the agency's wine expert had told him to do, thus liberating the esters and ethers, until his wife said, as she always did, it being the standard toast in her parents' home, "Cheers, dears!"

Rebecca continued the story of her first apartment. Jacques had never worked. Georgene never held a job more than three weeks. The three of them contributed to a kitty, to which all enjoyed equal access. Rebecca had a separate bedroom. Jacques and Georgene sometimes worked on television scripts; they pinned the bulk of their hopes onto a serial titled *The IBI*—"I" for Intergalactic, or Interplanetary, or something—*in Space and Time*. One of their friends was a young Communist who never washed and always had money because his father owned half of the West Side. During the day, when the two girls were off working, Jacques flirted with a young Swede upstairs who kept dropping her mop onto the tiny balcony outside their window. "A real bombardier," Rebecca said. When Rebecca moved into a single apartment for herself and was all settled and happy, Georgene and Jacques offered to bring a mattress and sleep on her floor. Rebecca felt that the time had come for her to put her foot down. She said no. Later, Jacques married a girl other than Georgene.

"Cashews, anybody?" Richard said. He had bought a can at the corner delicatessen, expressly for this visit, though if Rebecca had not been coming, he would have bought something else there on some other excuse, just for the pleasure of buying his first thing at the store where in the coming years he would purchase so much and become so well known.

"No thank you," Rebecca said. Richard was so
far from expecting refusal that out of momentum
he pressed them on her again exclaiming, "Please!
They're so good for you." She took two and bit one
in half.

He offered the dish, a silver porringer given to the
Maples as a wedding present and which they had never
before had the space to unpack, to his wife, who took
a greedy handful and looked so pale that he asked,
"How do you feel?" not so much forgetting the presence of their guest as parading his concern, quite
genuine at that, before her.

"Fine," Joan said edgily, and perhaps she did.

Though the Maples told some stories—how they had
lived in a log cabin in a Y.M.C.A. camp for the first
three months of their married life, how Bitsy Flaner, a
mutual friend, was the only girl enrolled in Bentham
Divinity School, how Richard's advertising work
brought him into contact with Yogi Berra—they did
not regard themselves (that is, each other) as raconteurs, and Rebecca's slight voice dominated the talk.
She had a gift for odd things.

Her rich uncle lived in a metal house, furnished with
auditorium chairs. He was terribly afraid of fire. Right
before the depression he had built an enormous boat to
take himself and some friends to Polynesia. All his
friends lost their money in the crash. He did not. He
made money. He made money out of everything. But
he couldn't go on the trip alone, so the boat was still

waiting in Oyster Bay, a huge thing, rising thirty feet out of water. The uncle was a vegetarian. Rebecca had not eaten turkey for Thanksgiving until she was thirteen years old because it was the family custom to go to the uncle's house on that holiday. The custom was dropped during the war, when the children's synthetic heels made black marks all over his asbestos floor. Rebecca's family had not spoken to the uncle since. "Yes, what got me," Rebecca said, "was the way each new wave of vegetables would come in as if it were a different course."

Richard poured the sherry around again and, because this made him the center of attention anyway, said, "Don't some vegetarians have turkeys molded out of crushed nuts for Thanksgiving?"

After a stretch of silence, Joan said, "I don't know." Her voice, unused for ten minutes, cracked on the last syllable. She cleared her throat, scraping Richard's heart.

"What would they stuff them with?" Rebecca asked, dropping an ash into the saucer beside her.

Beyond and beneath the window there arose a clatter. Joan reached the windows first, Richard next, and lastly Rebecca, standing on tiptoe, elongating her neck. Six mounted police, standing in their stirrups, were galloping two abreast down Thirteenth Street. When the Maples' exclamations had subsided, Rebecca remarked, "They do it every night at this time. They seem awfully jolly, for policemen."

"Oh, and it's snowing!" Joan cried. She was pathetic

about snow; she loved it so much, and in these last years had seen so little. "On our first night here! Our first *real* night." Forgetting herself, she put her arms around Richard, and Rebecca, where another guest might have turned away, or smiled too broadly, too encouragingly, retained without modification her sweet, absent look and studied, through the embracing couple, the scene outdoors. The snow was not taking on the wet street; only the hoods and tops of parked automobiles showed an accumulation.

"I think I'd best go," Rebecca said.

"Please don't," Joan said with an urgency Richard had not expected; clearly she was very tired. Probably the new home, the change in the weather, the good sherry, the currents of affection between herself and her husband that her sudden hug had renewed, and Rebecca's presence had become in her mind the inextricable elements of one enchanting moment.

"Yes, I think I'll go because you're so snuffly and peakèd."

"Can't you just stay for one more cigarette? Dick, pass the sherry around."

"A teeny bit," Rebecca said, holding out her glass. "I guess I told you, Joan, about the boy I went out with who pretended to be a headwaiter."

Joan giggled expectantly. "No, honestly, you never did." She hooked her arm over the back of the chair and wound her hand through the slats, like a child assuring herself that her bedtime has been postponed. "What did he do? He imitated headwaiters?"

"Yes, he was the kind of guy who, when we get out

of a taxi and there's a grate giving out steam, crouches down"—Rebecca lowered her head and lifted her arms—"and pretends he's the Devil."

The Maples laughed, less at the words themselves than at the way Rebecca had evoked the situation by conveying, in her understated imitation, both her escort's flamboyant attitude and her own undemonstrative nature. They could see her standing by the taxi door, gazing with no expression as her escort bent lower and lower, seized by his own joke, his fingers writhing demonically as he felt horns sprout through his scalp, flames lick his ankles, and his feet shrivel into hoofs. Rebecca's gift, Richard realized, was not that of having odd things happen to her but that of representing, through the implicit contrast with her own sane calm, all things touching her as odd. This evening too might appear grotesque in her retelling: "Six policemen on horses galloped by and she cried 'It's snowing!' and hugged him. He kept telling her how sick she was and filling us full of sherry."

"What else did he do?" Joan asked.

"At the first place we went to—it was a big night club on the roof of somewhere—on the way out he sat down and played the piano until a woman at a harp asked him to stop."

Richard asked, "Was the woman *playing* the harp?"

"Yes, she was strumming away." Rebecca made circular motions with her hands.

"Well, did he play the tune she was playing? Did he *accompany* her?" Petulance, Richard realized without understanding why, had entered his tone.

"No, he just sat down and played something else. I couldn't tell what it was."

"Is this *really* true?" Joan asked, egging her on.

"And then at the next place we went to, we had to wait at the bar for a table and I looked around and he was walking among the tables asking people if everything was all right."

"Wasn't it *awful?*" said Joan.

"Yes. Later he played the piano there, too. We were sort of the main attraction. Around midnight he thought we ought to go out to Brooklyn to his sister's house. I was exhausted. We got off the subway two stops too early, under the Manhattan Bridge. It was deserted, with nothing going by except black limousines. Miles above our head"—she stared up, as though at a cloud, or the sun—"was the Manhattan Bridge and he kept saying it was the el. We finally found some steps and two policemen who told us to go back to the subway."

"What does this amazing man do for a living?" Richard asked.

"He teaches school. He's quite bright." She stood up, extending in stretch a long, silvery white arm. Richard got her coat and said he'd walk her home.

"It's only three-quarters of a block," Rebecca protested in a voice free of any insistent inflection.

"You must walk her home, Dick," Joan said. "Pick up a pack of cigarettes." The idea of his walking in the snow seemed to please her, as if she were anticipating how he would bring back with him, in the snow on his shoulders and the coldness of his face, all the sensations of the walk she was not well enough to risk.

"You should stop smoking for a day or two," he told her.

Joan waved them goodbye from the head of the stairs.

The snow, invisible except around street lights, exerted a fluttering romantic pressure on their faces. "Coming down hard now," he said.

"Yes."

At the corner, where the snow gave the green light a watery blueness, her hesitancy in following him as he turned to walk with the light across Thirteenth Street led him to ask, "It is this side of the street you live on, isn't it?"

"Yes."

"I thought I remembered from the time we drove you down from Boston." The Maples had been living in the West Eighties then. "I remember I had an impression of big buildings."

"The church and the butcher's school," Rebecca said. "Every day about ten when I'm going to work the boys learning to be butchers come out for an intermission all bloody and laughing."

Richard looked up at the church; the steeple was fragmentarily silhouetted against the scattered lit windows of a tall improvement on Seventh Avenue. "Poor church," he said. "It's hard in this city for a steeple to be the tallest thing."

Rebecca said nothing, not even her habitual "Yes." He felt rebuked for being preachy. In his embarrassment he directed her attention to the first next thing he saw, a poorly lettered sign above a great door. "Food Trades Vocational High School," he read aloud. "The people upstairs told us that the man before the man before *us* in our apartment was a wholesale meat salesman who called himself a Purveyor of Elegant Foods. He kept a woman in the apartment."

"Those big windows up there," Rebecca said, pointing up at the third story of a brownstone, "face mine across the street. I can look in and feel we are neighbors. Someone's always there; I don't know what they do for a living."

After a few more steps they halted, and Rebecca, in a voice that Richard imagined to be slightly louder than her ordinary one, said, "Do you want to come up and see where I live?"

"Sure." It seemed implausible to refuse.

They descended four concrete steps, opened a shabby orange door, entered an overheated half-basement lobby, and began to climb four flights of wooden stairs. Richard's suspicion on the street that he was trespassing beyond the public gardens of courtesy turned to certain guilt. Few experiences so savor of the illicit as mounting stairs behind a woman's fanny. Three years ago, Joan had lived in a fourth-floor walkup, in Cambridge. Richard never took her home, even when the whole business, down to the last intimacy, had become formula, without the fear that the landlord, justifiably furious, would leap from his door and devour him as they passed.

Opening her door, Rebecca said, "It's hot as hell in here," swearing for the first time in his hearing. She turned on a weak light. The room was small; slanting planes, the underside of the building's roof, intersecting the ceiling and walls, cut large prismatic volumes from Rebecca's living space. As he moved further forward, toward Rebecca, who had not yet removed her coat, Richard perceived, on his right, an unexpected area created where the steeply slanting roof extended itself to the floor. Here a double bed was placed. Tightly bounded on three sides, the bed had the appearance not so much of a piece of furniture as of a permanently installed, blanketed platform. He quickly took his eyes from it and, unable to face Rebecca at once, stared at two kitchen chairs, a metal bridge lamp around the rim of whose shade plump fish and helm wheels alternated, and a four-shelf bookcase—all of which, being slender and proximate to a tilting wall, had an air of threatened verticality.

"Yes, here's the stove on top of the refrigerator I told you about," Rebecca said. "Or did I?"

The top unit overhung the lower by several inches on all sides. He touched his fingers to the stove's white side. "This room is quite sort of nice," he said.

"Here's the view," she said. He moved to stand beside her at the windows, lifting aside the curtains and peering through tiny flawed panes into the apartment across the street.

"That guy *does* have a huge window," Richard said.

She made a brief agreeing noise of n's.

Though all the lamps were on, the apartment across the street was empty. "Looks like a furniture store," he said. Rebecca had still not taken off her coat. "The snow's keeping up."

"Yes. It is."

"Well"—this word was too loud; he finished the sentence too softly—"thanks for letting me see it. I—have you read this?" He had noticed a copy of *Auntie Mame* lying on a hassock.

"I haven't had the time," she said.

"I haven't read it either. Just reviews. That's all I ever read."

This got him to the door. There, ridiculously, he turned. It was only at the door, he decided in retrospect, that her conduct was quite inexcusable: not only did she stand unnecessarily close, but, by shifting the weight of her body to one leg and leaning her head sidewise, she lowered her height several inches, placing him in a dominating position exactly fitted to the broad, passive shadows she must have known were on her face.

"Well—" he said.

"Well." Her echo was immediate and possibly meaningless.

"Don't, don't let the b-butchers get you." The stammer of course ruined the joke, and her laugh, which had begun as soon as she had seen by his face that he would attempt something funny, was completed ahead of his utterance.

As he went down the stairs she rested both hands on the banister and looked down toward the next landing. "Good night," she said.

"Night." He looked up; she had gone into her room. Oh but they were close.

Who Made Yellow
Roses Yellow?

OF THE THREE TELEPHONES IN THE APARTMENT, THE ONE
in the living room rested on a tabouret given to Fred
Platt's grandmother by Henry James, who considered
her, the Platts claimed, the only educated woman in
the United States. Above this cherrywood gift hung
an oval mirror, its frame a patterned involvement of
cherubs, acanthus leaves, and half-furled scrolls; its
gilt, smooth as butter in the valleys between figures,
yielded on the crests of the relief to touches of Wat-
teau brown. Great-Uncle Randy, known for his
whims and mustaches, had rescued the mirror from a
Paris auction. In the capacious room there was nothing
of no intrinsic interest, nothing that would not serve
as cause for a narrative, except the three overstuffed

pieces installed by Fred's father—two chairs, facing each other at a distance of three strides, and a crescent-shaped sofa, all covered in spandy-new, navy-blue leather. This blue, the dark warm wood of inherited cabinets, the twilight colors of aged books, the scarlet and purple of the carpet from Cairo (where Charlotte, Uncle Randy's wife, had caught a bug and died), and the dismal sonorities of the Secentistico Transfiguration on the west wall vibrated around the basal shade of plum. Plum: a color a man can rest in, the one toward which all dressing gowns tend. Reinforcing the repose and untroubled finality of the interior were the several oval shapes. The mirror was one of a family, kin to the feminine ellipse of the coffee table; to the burly arc of Daddy's sofa, as they never failed to call it; to the ovoid, palely painted base of a Florentine lamp; to the plaster medallion on the ceiling—the one cloud in the sky of the room—and the recurrent, tiny gold seal of the Oxford University Press, whose books, monochrome and Latinate as dons, were among the chief of the senior Platt's plum-colored pleasures.

Fred, his only son, age twenty-five, dialled a JUdson number. He listened to five burrs before the receiver was picked up, exposing the tail end of a girl's giggle. Still tittery, she enunciated, "Carson Chemi-cal."

"Hello. Is—ah, Clayton Thomas Clayton there, do you know?"

"Mr. Thomas Clayton? Yes he is. Just one moment please." So poor Clayton Clayton had finally got somebody to call him by his middle name, that "Thomas" which his parents must have felt made all the difference between the absurd and the sublime.

"Mr. Clayton's of-fice," another girl said. "About what was it you wished to speak to him?"

"Well nothing, really. It's a friend."

"Just one moment, please."

After a delay—purely disciplinary, Fred believed—an unexpectedly deep and even melodious voice said, "Yes?"

"Clayton Clayton?"

A pause. "Who is this?"

"Good morning, sir. I represent the Society for the Propagation and Eventual Adoption of the A. D. Spooner Graduated Income Tax Plan. As perhaps you know, this plan calls for an income tax which increases in inverse proportion to income, so that the wealthy are exempted and the poor taxed out of existence. Within five years, Mr. Spooner estimates, poverty would be eliminated: within ten, a thing not even of memory. Word has come to our office—"

"It's Fred Platt, isn't it?"

"Word has come to our office that in recent years Providence has so favored thee as to incline thy thoughts the more favorably to the Plan."

"Fred?"

"Congratulations. You now own the Motorola combination phonograph-and-megaphone. Do you care to try for the Bendix?"

"How long have you been in town? It's damn good to hear from you."

"Since April first. It's a prank of my father's. Who are all these girls you live in the midst of?"

"Your father called you back?"

"I'm not sure. I keep forgetting to look up 'wastrel' in the dictionary."

That made Clayton laugh. "I thought you were studying at the Sorbonne."

"I was, I was."

"But you're not now."

"I'm not now. *Moi et la Sorbonne, nous sommes kaput.*" When the other was silent, Fred added, "*Beaucoup kaput.*"

"Look, we must get together," Clayton said.

"Yes. I was wondering if you eat lunch."

"When had you thought?"

"Soon?"

"Wait. I'll check." Some muffled words—a question with his hand over the mouthpiece. A drawer scraped. "Say Fred, this is bad. I have something on the go every day this week."

"So. Well, what about June 21st? They say the solstice will be lovely this year."

"Wait. What about today? I'm free today, they just told me."

"Today?" Fred had to see Clayton soon, but immediately seemed like a push. "*Comme vous voulez, Monsieur.* Oneish?"

"All right, uh—could you make it twelve-thirty? I have a good bit to do . . ."

"Just as easy. There's a Chinese place on East Forty-ninth Street run by Australians. Excellent murals of Li Po embracing the moon in the Yalu, *plus* the coronation of Henri Quatre."

"I wonder, could that be done some other time? As I

say, there's some stuff here at the office. Do you know Shulman's? It's on Third Avenue, a block from here, so that—"

"Press of work, eh?"

"You said it," Clayton said, evidently sensing no irony. "Then I'll see you then."

"In all the old de dum de dumpty that this heart of mine embraces."

"Pardon?"

"See you then."

"Twelve-thirty at Shulman's."

"Absolutely."

"So long."

"So long."

The first impulse after a humiliation is to look into a mirror. The heavy Parisian looking glass, hung on too long a wire, leaned inches from the wall. A person standing would see reflected in it not his head but the carpet, some furniture, and perhaps, in the upper portion of the oval, his shoes and cuffs. By tilting his chair Fred could see his face, flushed like the mask someone momentarily absent from an enervating cocktail party spies in the bathroom mirror. There, the hot-skinned head, backed by pastel tiles and borrowing imperturability from the porcelain fixtures, strikes the owner as a glamorous symbol of Man, half angel, half beast; and each eye seems the transparent base of a cone luminous with intuitions, secrets, quips, deviltry, and love. Here, in this overstuffed room, his red face, above his black suit, just looked hot. His excited appearance annoyed him. Between his feverish attempt to rekindle friendship—his mind skidding, his tongue wagging—and Clayton's response an embarrassing and degrading disproportion had existed.

Until now it had seemed foolishly natural for Clayton to offer him a job. Reportedly he had asked Bim Blackwood to jump Harcourt for a publicity job at Carson Chemical. Bim had said, without seeing anything funny in the word, that Clayton had lots of "power" at Carson. "In just three years, he's near the top. He's a *killer*. Really."

It had been hard to gather from Bim's description exactly what Clayton did. As Bim talked on, flicking with increasing rapidity at the stiff eave of brown hair that overhung his forehead with conceited carelessness, he would say anything to round out a sentence, never surrendering his right to be taken seriously. "It's an octopus," he had asserted. "You know *ev*erything is chemicals *ulti*mately. Clayton told me the first thing he was given to do was help design the wrapper for an ammoniated chewing gum they were just putting out. He said the big question was whether chalk-white or mint-green suggested better a clean feeling in the mouth. They had a survey on it; it cost thousands and *thousands*—thousands of little men going inside people's mouths. Of course he doesn't draw any more; he consults. Can you imagine doing nothing all day but *consult?* On pamphlets, you know, and 'flyers'—what *are* flyers anyway?—and motion pictures to show to salesmen to show them how to explain the things they sell. He's *ter*ribly involved with *tele*vision; he told me a *hor*rible story about a play about Irish peasants the Carson Chemical Hour was

: 87 :

putting on and at the last minute it dawned on everybody that these people were *organic farmers*. Clayton Clayton saw it through. The killer instinct."

Clayton hadn't had to go into the Army. Troubled knees, or something. That was the thing about poor children: they acquired disabilities which give them the edge in later life. It's cruel, to expect a man without a handicap to go far.

Fred's position was not desperate. An honorable office in the investments firm (for Father was of the newest school, which sees no wrong in playing favorites) was not, as Father had said, with his arch way of trotting out cliches as if they were moderately obscure literary quotations, "the fate worse than death." Furthermore—he was a great man for furthermores—anyone who imagined that the publicity arm of Carson Chemical was an ivory tower compared to Braur, Chappell & Platt lived in a fool's paradise.

Yet viewed allegorically the difference seemed great. Something about all this, perhaps the chaste spring greenery of Central Park, which from these windows was spread out with the falcon's-eye perspective of a medieval map, suggested one of those crossroads in *The Faerie Queene*.

Besides, he had been very kind to Clayton—gotten him onto the *Quaff*, really. Sans *Quaff*, where would Clayton be? Not that Clayton need consider any of this. Hell, it wasn't as if Fred were asking for something; he was offering something. He pushed back the chair a few feet—so a full view of himself was available in the tilted mirror: a tall, ascetic youth, dressed in darkest gray. A lapsed Episcopalian, Fred was half in love with the clergy.

Entering, late, the appointed restaurant, Fred instantly spotted Clayton Clayton standing at the bar. That three years had passed, that the place was smoky and crowded with interchangeable men, did not matter; an eclipsing head bowed, and the fragment of cheek then glimpsed, though in itself nothing but a daub of white, not only communicated to Fred one human identity but stirred in him warm feelings for the *Quaff*, college, his youth generally, and even America. Fred had inherited that trick of the rich of seeming to do everything out of friendship, but he was three generations removed from the making of the money, and a manner of business had become, in him, a way of life; his dealings were in fact at the mercy of his affections. Grotesquely close to giggling, he walked up to his man and intoned, *"Ego sum via, vita, veritas."*

Clayton turned, grinned, and pumped Fred's hand. "How *are* you, Fred?"

Members of the *Quaff* did not ask one another how they were; Fred had supposed ex-members also did not. Finding they did baffled him. He could not think of the joke to turn such simple attack aside. "Pretty well," he conceded and, as if these words were an exorcism enabling the gods of fatuity to descend and dwell in his lips, heard himself add, in what seemed full solemnity, "How are *you?*"

"I'm doing"—Clayton paused, nodding once, giving the same words a new import—"pretty well."

"Yes, everybody says."

"I was glad I could make it today. I really am up to my ears this week." Confidingly: "I'm in a crazy business."

On one wall of the restaurant were Revolutionary murals, darkened perhaps by smoke and time but more likely by the painter's caution. "Ah," said Fred, gesturing. "The Renaissance Popes in Hell."

"Would you like one of these?" Clayton touched the glass in front of him; it contained that collegiate brew, beer.

How tender of Clayton still to drink beer! By a trick of vision the liquid stood unbounded by glass. The sight of that suspended amber cylinder, like his magic first glimpse of Clayton's face, conjured in Fred a sensation of fondness. This time he curbed his tendency to babble and said, anxious to be honest, certain that the merest addition of the correct substance—the simple words exchanged by comrades—would reform the alchemy of the relationship, "Yes. I would like one. Quite a bit."

"I tell you. Let's grab a table and order from there. They'll let us stand here all day."

Fred felt not so much frustrated as deflected, as if the glass that wasn't around the beer was around Clayton.

"There's a table." Clayton picked up his stein, placed a half dollar in the center of the circle its base had occupied, and shouldered away from the bar. He led the way into a booth, past two old men brandishing their topcoats. Inside, the high partitions shielded them from much of the noise of the place. Clayton took two menus from behind the sugar and handed one to Fred. "We had better order the food first, then ask for the beer. If you asked for the drinks first, they'll just run off." He was perfect: the medium-short dry-combed hair, the unimpeachable brown suit, the buttonless collar, the genially dragged vowels, the little edges of efficiency bracing the consonants. Some traces of the scholarship-bothered freshman from Hampton (Md.) High School who had come down to the *Quaff* on Candidates' Night with an armful of framed sports cartoons remained—the not smoking, the tucked-in chin and the attendant uplook of the boyishly lucid eyes, and the skin allergy that placed on the flank of each jaw a constellation of red dots. Even these vestiges fitted into the picture, by lending him, until he learned to feign it, the ingratiating uncertainty desired in New York executives. It was just this suggestion of inexperience that in his genuine inexperience Clayton was working to suppress. "See anything you like," he asked with a firmness not interrogative.

"I think maybe a lamb chop."

"I don't see them on the menu."

"I don't either."

Raising his hand to the level of his ear and snapping his fingers, Clayton summoned a waiter. "This gentleman wants a lamb chop. Do you have them?"

The waiter didn't bother to answer, just wrote it down.

"I think I might try," Clayton went on, "the chopped sirloin with mushroom sauce. Beans instead of the peas, if you will. And I'm having another glass of Ballantine. Shall I make that two, Fred?"

"Do you have any decent German beer? Würz-burger? Or Löwenbräu?"

The request materialized the man, who had been serving them with only his skimpy professional self. Now he smiled, and stood bodied forth as a great-boned Teuton in the prime of his fifties, with the square Bavarian skull, a short hooked nose, and portentous ears covered with a diaphanous fuzz that brought to the dignity they already possessed a certain silky glamour. "I believe, sir, we have the Löwenbräu. I don't think we have any of the Würzburger, sir."

"O.K. Anything." Though Fred truly repented stealing Clayton's show, the evidence of his crime refused to disappear. He had called into being a genie—cloying, zealous, delighted to have his cavernous reserve of attentiveness tapped at last. The waiter bowed and indeed whispered, making an awkward third party of Clayton, "I think we have the Löwenbräu. If not, would an English stout do? A nice Guinness, sir?"

"Anything is fine." Trying to bring Clayton back into it, Fred asked him, "Do you want one? Fewer bubbles than Ballantine. Less tingle for more ferment."

Clayton's answering laugh would have been agreeable if he had not, while uttering it, lowered his eyelids, showing that he conceived of this as a decision whereby he stood to gain or lose. "No, I think I'll stick to Ballantine." He looked Fred needlessly in the eyes. When Clayton felt threatened, the middle sector of his face clouded over; the area between his brows and nostrils queerly condensed.

Fred was both repelled and touched. The expression

was exactly that worn by the adolescent Clayton at the *Quaff* candidates' punches, when all the dues members, dead to the magazine, showed up resplendent in black suits and collar pins, eager for Martinis, as full of chatter and strut as a flock of whooping cranes bent on proving they were not extinct yet. Fred pitied Clayton, remembering the days when Fred alone, a respected if sophomore member, was insisting that the kid with the gag name be elected to the *Quaff:* The point was he could draw. Wonky, sure. He was right out of the funny papers. But at least his hands looked like hands. Outrageous, of course, to have the drawings framed, but his parents put him up to that—anybody who'd call a helpless baby Clayton Clayton. . . . He wore cocoa-colored slacks and sport shirts. They'd wear out. If he was sullen, he was afraid. The point was, If we don't get anybody on the magazine who can draw we'll be forced to run daguerreotypes of Chester Arthur and the Conkling Gang.

"Do you see much of Anna Spooner?" Clayton asked, referring back, perhaps unconsciously, to Fred's earlier mistake, his mention of the income-tax plan of their friend A. D. Spooner, nicknamed "Anno Domini" and eventually "Anna."

"Once or twice. I haven't been back that long. He said he kept running into you at the Old Grads' Marching Society."

"Once in a while."

"You don't sound too enthusiastic."

"I hadn't meant to. I mean I hadn't meant not to. He's about the same. Same tie, same jokes. He never thanks me when I buy him a drink. I don't mean the money bothers me. It's one of those absurd little things. I shouldn't even mention it."

The waiter brought the beers. Fred stared into his Löwenbräu and breathed the word "Yeah."

"How long *have* you been back?"

"Two weeks, I guess."

"That's right. You said. Well, tell me about it. What've you been doing for three years?" His hands were steadily folded on the table, conference-style. "I'm interested."

Fred laughed outright at him. "There isn't that much. In the Army I was in Germany in the Quartermaster Corps."

"What did you do?"

"Nothing. Typed. Played blackjack, faro, Rook."

"Do you find it's changed you much?"

"I type faster. And my chest now is a mass of pornographic tattoos."

Clayton laughed a little. "It just interests me. I know that psychologically the effect on me of *not* going in is —is genuine. I feel not exactly guilty, but it's something that everyone of our generation has gone through. Not to seems incom*plete*."

"It should, it should. I bet you can't even rev out a Bowling Bunting H-4 jet-cycle tetrameter. As for shooting a bazooka! Talk of St. Teresa's spiritual experiences—"

"It's impressive, how little it's changed you. I wonder if I'm changed. I do like the work, you know. People are always slamming advertising, but I've found out it's a pretty damn essential thing in our economy."

The waiter came and set their platters before them. Clayton set to with a disconcerting intensity, forking in the food as often with his left hand as his right, pausing only to ask questions. "Then you went back to Europe."

"Then I went back to Europe."

"Why? I mean what did you do? Did you do any writing?"

In recent years Fred's literary intelligence had exerted itself primarily in the invention of impeccable but fruitless puns. Parcel Proust. Or Supple Simon. (Supple Simon met a Neiman/Fellow at the Glee Club, gleamin'./Said Supple Simon, "Tell me, Fellow/Who made yellow roses yellow?") "Why, yes," he told Clayton. "Quite a bit. I've just completed a three-volume biography of the great Hungarian actress, Juxta Pose."

"No, actually. What did you do in Paris?"

"Actually, I sat in a chair. The same chair whenever I could. It was a straw chair in the sidewalk area of a restaurant on the Boulevard Saint-Michel. In the summer and spring the tables are in the open, but when it gets cold they enclose the area with large windows. It's best then. Everybody except you sits inside the restaurant, where it's warm. It's best of all at breakfast, around eleven of a nippy morning, with your *café* and *croissant avec du beurre* and your *coude* all on a little table the size of a tray, and people outside the window trying to sell *ballons* to Christmas tourists."

"You must know French perfectly. It annoys hell out of me that I don't know any."

"*Oui, pardon, zut!* and *alors!* are all you need for ordinary conversation. Say them after me: *oui*—the lips so—*par-don*—"

"The reason you probably don't write more," Clayton said, "is that you have too much taste. Your critical sense is always a jump ahead of your creative urge." Getting no response, he went on, "I haven't been doing much drawing, either. Except roughing out ideas. But I plan to come back to it."

"I know you do. I know you will."

That was what Clayton wanted to hear. He loved work; it was all he knew how to do. His type saw competition as the spine of the universe. His *Quaff* career had been all success, all adaptation and good sense, so that in his senior year Clayton was president, and everybody said he alone was keeping silly old *Quaff* alive, when in fact the club, with its fragile ethic of worthlessness, had withered under him.

Clayton had a forkful of hamburger poised between the plate and his mouth. "What does your father want?" In went the hamburger.

"My father seems to fascinate you. He is a thin man in his late fifties. He sits at one end of an enormous long room filled with priceless things. He is wearing a purple dressing gown and trying to read a book. But he feels the room is tipping. So he wants me to get in there with him and sit at the other end to keep the balance."

"No. I didn't mean—"

"He wants me to get a job. Know of one?" So the crucial question was out, stated like a rebuke.

Clayton carefully chewed. "What sort?"

"I've already been offered a position in Braur, Chappell & Platt. A fine old firm. I'm looking for something with less pay."

"In publishing?"

Stalling, stalling. "Or advertising."

Clayton set down his fork. "Gee. You should be able to get something."

"I wouldn't know why. I have no experience. I can't use my father's pull. That wouldn't be the game."

"I wish you had been here about six months ago. There was an opening up at Carson, and I asked Bim Blackwood, but he didn't want to make the jump. Speaking of Bim, he's certainly come along."

"Come along? Where to?"

"You know. He seems more mature. I feel he's gotten ahold of himself. His view of things is better proportioned."

"That's very perceptive. Who else do we know who's come along?"

"Well, I would say Harry Ducloss has. I was talking last week with a man Harry works for."

"He said he's come along?"

"He said he thought highly of him."

" 'Thought highly.' Fermann was always thinking highly of people."

"I saw Fermann in the street the other day. Boy!"

"Not coming along?"

Clayton lifted his wrists so the waiter could clear away his plate. "It's just, it's"—with a peculiar intensity, as if Fred had often thought the same thing but never so well expressed it—"*something* to see those tin gods again."

"Would you young men like dessert?" the waiter asked. "Coffee?" To Fred: "We have nice freshly baked strudel. Very nice. It's made right in the kitchen ovens."

Fred deferred to Clayton. "Do you have time for coffee?"

Clayton craned his neck to see the clock. "Eight of two." He looked at Fred apologetically. "To tell the truth—"

"No coffee," Fred told the waiter.

"Oh, let's have it. It'll take just a few minutes."

"No, it doesn't matter to me and I don't want you to be late."

"They won't miss me. I'm not *that* indispensable. Are you sure you don't want any?"

"Positive."

"All right," Clayton said in the dragged-out, musical tone of a parent acceding to a demand that will only do the child harm. "Could I have the check, please, waiter?"

"Certainly, sir." The something sarcastic about that "sir" was meant for Fred to see.

The check came to $3.79. When Fred reached for his wallet, Clayton said, "Keep that in your pocket. This is on me."

"Don't be a fool. The lunch was my idea."

"No, please. Let me take this."

Fred dropped a five-dollar bill on the table.

"No, look," Clayton said. "I know you have the money—"

"Money! We *all* have money."

Clayton, at last detecting anger, looked up timidly, his irises in the top of his eyes, his chin tucked in. "Please. You were always quite kind to me."

It was like a plain girl opening her mouth in the middle of a kiss. Fred wordlessly took back his five. Clayton handed four ones and a quarter to the waiter and said, "That's right."

"Thank *you*, sir."

"Thanks a lot," Fred said to Clayton as they moved toward the door.

"It's—" Clayton shook his head slightly. "You can get the next one."

"*Merci beaucoup.*"

"I hope you didn't mind coming to this place."

"A great place. Vy, sey sought I vuss Cherman."

Outside, the pavement glittered as if cement were precious; Third Avenue, disencumbered of the el, seemed as spacious and queenly as a South American boulevard. In the harsh light of the two o'clock sun, blemishes invisible in the shadows of the restaurant could be noticed on the skin of Clayton's face—an uneven redness on the flesh of the nose, two spots on his forehead, a flaky area partially hidden beneath an eyebrow. Clayton's feet tended to shuffle backward; he was conscious of his skin, or anxious to get back to work. Fred stood still, making it clear he was travelling in another direction. Clayton did not feel free to go. "You really want a job in advertising?"

"Forget it. I don't really."

"I'll keep on the lookout."

"Don't go to any trouble, but thanks anyway."

"Thank *you*, for heaven's sake. I really enjoyed this. It's been good."

For a moment Fred was sorry; he had an impulse to walk a distance with Clayton, to forgive everything, but Clayton, helplessly offensive, smiled and said, "Well. Back to the salt mines."

"Well put." Fred lifted his hand in a benign ministerial gesture startling to passersby. "Ye are the salt of the earth. *La lumière du monde*. The light of the world. *Fils de Saint Louis, montez au ciel!*"

Clayton, bewildered by the foreign language, backed a step away and with an uncertain jerk of his hand affirmed, "See you."

"*Oui. Le roi est un bon homme. Le crayon de ma tante est sur la table de mon chat. Merci. Merci.* Meaning thank you. Thanks again."

Sunday Teasing

Sunday morning: waking, he felt long as a galaxy, and just lacked the will to get up, to unfurl the great sleepy length beneath the covers and go be disillusioned in the ministry by some servile, peace-of-mind-peddling preacher. If it wasn't peace of mind, it was the integrated individual, and if it wasn't the integrated individual, it was the power hidden within each one of us. Never a stern old commodity like sin or remorse, never an open-faced superstition. So he decided, without pretending that it was the preferable course as well as the easier, to stay home and read Saint Paul.

His wife fussed around the apartment with a too determined silence; whenever he read the Bible, she acted as if he were playing solitaire without having first invited her to play rummy, or as if he were delivering an oblique attack on Jane Austen and Henry Green, whom she mostly read. Trying to bring her into the Sunday-morning club, he said, "Here's my

: 101 :

grandfather's favorite passage, First Corinthians eleven, verse three. 'But I would have you know, that the head of every man is Christ; and the head of the woman is the man; and the head of Christ is God.' He loved reading that to my mother. It infuriated her."

A mulish perplexity occupied Macy's usually bland features. "*What?* The head? The head of every man. What does 'the head' mean exactly? I'm sorry, I just don't understand."

If he had been able to answer her immediately, he would have done so with a smile, but, though the sense of "head" in the text was perfectly clear, he couldn't find a synonym. After a silence he said, "It's so obvious."

"Read me the passage again. I really didn't hear it."

"No," he said.

"Come on, please. 'The head of the man is God . . .' "

"No."

She abruptly turned and went into the kitchen. "All you do is tease," she said from in there. "You think it's so funny." He hadn't been teasing her at all, but her saying it put the idea into his head.

They were having a friend to the midday meal that Sunday, Leonard Byrne, a Jewish friend who, no matter what the discussion was about, turned it to matters of the heart and body. "Do you realize," he said halfway through the lamb chops, a minute after a round of remarks concerning the movie *Camille* had unexpectedly died, "that in our home it was nothing for my father to kiss me? When I'd come home from summer camp, he'd actually em*brace* me—physically embrace me. No inhibitions about it at all. In my home, it was *nothing* for men physically to show affection for one another. I remember my uncle when he came to visit had *no* inhibitions about warmly embracing my father. Now that's one thing I find repugnant, personally re*pug*nant, to me about the American home. That there is none of that. It's evident that the American male has some innate fear of being mistaken for a homosexual. But *why*, that's the interesting thing, *why* should he be so protective of his virility? Why shouldn't the American father kiss the American son, when it's done in Italy, in Russia, in France?"

"It's the pioneer," Macy said; she seldom volunteered her opinions, and in this case, Arthur felt, did it only to keep Leonard from running on and on and eventually embarrassing himself. Now she was stuck with the words "It's the pioneer," which, to judge from her face, were beginning to seem idiotic to her. "Those men *had* to be virile," she gamely continued, "they were out there alone."

"By the way," Leonard said, resting his elbow on the very edge of the table and tilting his head toward her, for suaveness, "do you know, it has been established beyond all doubt, that the American pioneer was a drunkard? But that's not the point. Yes, people say, 'the pioneer,' but I can't quite see how that affects me, as a second-generation American."

"But that's it," Arthur told him. "It doesn't. You just said yourself that your family wasn't American. They kissed each other. Now take me. *I'm* an American. Eleventh-generation German. White, Protestant, Gentile, small-town, middle-class. I am *pure* American.

And do you know, I have never seen my father kiss my mother. Never."

Leonard, of course, was outraged ("That's shocking," he said. "That is truly shocking"), but Macy's reaction was what Arthur had angled for. It was hard to separate her perturbation at the announcement from the perturbation caused by her not knowing if he was lying or not. "That's not true," she told Leonard, but then asked Arthur, "Is it?"

"Of course it's true," he said, talking more to Leonard than to Macy. "Our family dreaded body contact. Years went by without my touching my mother. When I went to college, she got into the habit of hugging me goodbye, and now does it whenever we go home. But in my teens, when she was younger, there was nothing of the sort."

"You know, Arthur, that really frightens me," Leonard said.

"Why? Why should it? It never occurred to my father to manhandle me. He used to carry me when I was little, but when I got too heavy, he stopped. Just like my mother stopped dressing me when I could do it myself." Arthur decided to push the proposition farther, since nothing he had said since "I have never seen my father kiss my mother" had aroused as much interest. "After a certain age, the normal American boy is raised by casual people who just see in him a source of income—movie-house managers, garage attendants, people in luncheonettes. The man who ran the luncheonette where I ate did nothing but cheat us out of our money and crab about the noise we made, but I loved that man like a father."

"That's *ter*rible, Arthur," Leonard said. "In my family we didn't really trust anybody outside the family. Not that we didn't have friends. We had lots of friends. But it wasn't quite the *same*. Macy, your mother kissed you, didn't she?"

"Oh, yes. All the time. And my father."

"Ah, but Macy's parents are atheists," Arthur said.

"They're Unitarians," she said.

Arthur continued, "Now to go back to your *why* this should be so. What do we know about the United States other than the fact that it was settled by pioneers? It is a Protestant country, perhaps the only one. It and Switzerland. Now what *is* Protestantism? A vision of attaining God with nothing but the mind. Nothing but the mind alone on a mountaintop."

"Yes, yes, of course. We know that," Leonard said, though in fact Arthur had just stated (he now remembered) not a definition of Protestantism but Chesterton's definition of Puritanism.

"In place of the bureaucratic, interceding Church," Arthur went on, trying to correct himself, flushing because his argument had urged him into the sacred groves of his mind, "Luther's notion of Christ is substituted. The reason why in Catholic countries everybody kisses each other is that it's a huge family— God is a family of three, the Church is a family of millions, even heretics are kind of black sheep of the family. Whereas the Protestant lives all by himself, inside of himself. *Sola fide.* Man *should* be lonely."

"Yes, yes," Leonard said, puzzling Arthur; he had meant the statements to be debatable.

Arthur felt his audience was bored, because they

were eating again, so he said, as a punch, "I know when we have kids I'm certainly not going to kiss Macy in front of them."

It was too harsh a thing to say, too bold; he was too excited. Macy said nothing, did not even look up, but her face was tense with an accusatory meekness.

"No, I don't mean that," Arthur said. "It's all lies, lies, lies, lies. My family was very close."

Macy said to Leonard softly, "Don't you believe it. He's been telling the truth."

"I know it," Leonard said. "I've always felt that about Arthur's home ever since I met him. I really have."

And though Leonard could console himself with this supposed insight, something uncongenial had been injected into the gathering, and he became depressed; his mood clouded the room, weighed on their temples like smog, and when, hours later, he left, both Arthur and Macy were unwilling to let him go because he had not had a good time. In a guilty spurt of hospitality, they chattered to him of future arrangements. Leonard walked down the stairs with his hat at an angle less jaunty than when he had come up those stairs—a somehow damp angle, as if he had confused his inner drizzle with a state of outer weather.

Suppertime came. Macy mentioned that she didn't feel well and couldn't eat a bite. Arthur put Benny Goodman's 1938 Carnegie Hall Concert on the record-player and, rousing his wife from the Sunday *Times*, insisted that she, who had been raised on Scarlatti and Purcell, take notice of Jess Stacy's classic piano solo on

"Sing, Sing, Sing," which he played twice, for her benefit. He prepared some chicken-with-rice soup for himself, mixing the can with just half a can of water, since it would be for only one person and need not be too much thinned. The soup, heated to a simmer, looked so flavorful that he asked Macy if she really didn't want any. She looked up and thought. "Just a cupful," she said, which left him enough to fill a large bowl—plenty, though not a luxurious plenitude.

"Mm. That was so good," she said after finishing.

"Feel better?"

"Slightly."

Macy was reading through a collection of short stories, and Arthur brought the rocking chair from the bedroom and joined her by the lamp, with his paperback copy of *The Tragic Sense of Life*. Here again she misunderstood him; he knew that his reading Unamuno depressed her, and he was reading the book not to depress her but to get the book finished and depress her no longer. She knew nothing of the contents except for his remark one time that according to the author the source of religion is the unwillingness to die, yet she was suspicious.

"Why don't you ever read anything except scary philosophy?" she asked him.

"It isn't scary," he said. "The man's a Christian, sort of."

"You should read some fiction."

"I will, I will as soon as I finish this."

Perhaps an hour passed. "Oh," Macy said, dropping her book to the floor. "That's *so* terrible, it's so *awful*."

He looked at her inquiringly. She was close to tears.

"There's a story in here," she explained. "It just makes you sick. I don't want to think about it."

"See, if you'd read Kierkegaard instead of squalid fiction—"

"No, really. I don't even think it's a good story, it's so awful."

He read the story himself, and Macy moved into the sling chair facing him. He was conscious of her body as clouds of pale color beyond the edge of the page, stirring with gentle unease, like a dawn. "Very good," Arthur said when he was done. "Quite moving."

"It's so horrible," Macy said. "Why was he so awful to his wife?"

"It's all explained. He was out of his caste. He was trapped. A perfectly nice man, corrupted by bad luck."

"How can you *say* that? That's so ridiculous."

"Ridiculous! Why Macy, the whole pathos of the story lies in the fact that the man, for all his selfishness and cruelty, loves the woman. After all, *he's* telling the story, and if the wife emerges as a sympathetic character, it's because that's the way he sees her. The description of her at the train—here. 'As the train glided away she turned toward me her face, calm and so sweet and which, in the instant before it vanished, appeared a radiant white heart.'" The story, clumsily translated from the French, was titled *Un Cœur Blanc*. "And then later, remembering—'It gladdens me that I was able then to simulate a depth of affection that I did not at that time feel. She too generously repaid me, and in that zealous response was there not her sort of victory?' That's absolutely sympathetic, you see. It's a terrific image—this perceptive man caged in his own weak character."

To his surprise, Macy had begun to cry. Tears mounted from the lower lids of eyes still looking at him. "Macy," he said, kneeling by her chair and touching his forehead to hers. He earnestly wished her well at that moment, yet his actions seemed hurried and morbid. "What is it? Of course I feel sorry for the woman."

"You said he was a *nice* man."

"I didn't mean it. I meant that the horror of the story lies in the fact that the man *does* understand, that he does love the woman."

"It just shows, it shows how *different* we are."

"No we're not. We're exactly alike. Our noses"—he touched hers, then his—"are alike as two peas, our mouths like two turnips, our chins like two hamsters." She laughed sobbingly, but the silliness of his refutation proved the truth of her remark.

He held her as long as her crying remained strenuous, and when it relented, she moved to the sofa and lay down, saying, "It's awful when you have an ache and don't know if it's your head or your ear or your tooth."

He put the palm of his hand on her forehead. He could never tell about fevers. Her skin felt warm, but then human beings were warm things. "Have you taken your temperature?"

"I don't know where the thermometer is. Broken, probably." She lay in a forsaken attitude, with one arm, the bluish underside uppermost, extended outward,

supported in midair by the limits of its flexure. "Oog,"
she said, sticking out her tongue. "This room is a mess."
The Bible had never been replaced in the row of books;
it lay on its side, spanning four secular volumes. Several
glasses, drained after dinner, stood like castle sentries
on the window sill, the mantel, and the lowest shelf of
the bookcase. Leonard had left his rubbers under the
table. The jacket of the Goodman record lay on the
rug, and the Sunday *Times*, that manifold summation
of a week's confusion, was oppressively everywhere.
Arthur's soup bowl was still on the table; Macy's cup,
cockeyed in the saucer, rested by her chair, along with
Unamuno and the collection of short stories. "It's always so awful," she said. "Why don't you ever help to
keep the room neat?"

"I will, I will. Now you go to bed." He guided her
into the other room and took her temperature. She
kept the thermometer in her mouth as she undressed
and got into her nightgown. He read her temperature
as 98.8°. "Very very slight," he told her. "I prescribe
sleep."

"I look so pale," she said in front of the bathroom
mirror.

"We never should have discussed *Camille*." When she
was in bed, her face pink against the white pillow and
the rest of her covered, he said, "You and Garbo. Tell
me how Garbo says, 'You're fooling me.' "

"You're fooling me," she said in a fragile Swedish
whisper.

Back in the living room, Arthur returned the books
to the shelves, tearing even strips from the *Times* garden section as bookmarks. He assembled the newspa-

per and laid it on a window sill. He stood holding Leonard's rubbers for ten seconds, then dropped them in a corner. He took the record off the phonograph, slipped it into its envelope, and hid it in the closet with the others.

Lastly, he collected the dishes and glasses and washed them. As he stood at the sink, his hands in water which, where the suds thinned and broke, showed a silvery gray, the Sunday's events repeated themselves in his mind, bending like nacreous flakes around a central infrangible irritant, becoming the perfect and luminous thought: *You don't know anything.*

His Finest Hour

First they heard, at eight p.m., the sound of a tumbler shattering. It was a distinct noise, tripartite: the crack of the initial concussion, the plump, vegetal *pop* of the disintegration, and the gossip of settling fragments. The glass might have been hurled within their own living room. To George this showed how thin the walls were. The walls were thin, the ceiling flaked, the furniture smelled lewd, the electricity periodically failed. The rooms were tiny, the rent was monstrous, the view was dull. George Chandler hated New York City. A native of Arizona, he felt that the unclear air here was crowded with spirits constantly cheating him. As the sincere Christian examines each occurrence for the fingerprints of the Providential hand, George read into each irregular incident—a greeting in the subway, an unscheduled knock on the door—possible financial loss. His rule was, sit tight. This he did, not raising his eyes from the book with which he was teaching himself Arabic.

Rosalind, taller than her husband and less cautious, uncrossed her long legs and said, "Mrs. Irva must have dropsy."

George didn't want to talk about it, but he could seldom resist correcting her. "That wasn't dropped, honey. It was thrown."

Within the Irvas' rooms something wooden overturned, and it seemed a barrel was being rocked. "What do you suppose is wrong?" Rosalind had no book in her hand; evidently she had just been sitting there on the edge of the easy chair, waiting for something to listen to. She minded New York less than George. He hadn't noticed when she had come in from the dishes in the kitchenette. After supper every evening, he had his Arabic hour; during it he liked to be undisturbed. "Do you suppose something's the matter?" Rosalind persisted, slightly rephrasing her question in case he had heard it the first time.

George lowered his book with visible patience. "Does Irva drink?"

"I don't know. He's a chef."

"You think chefs don't drink. Just eat."

"I hadn't meant the two to be connected." Rosalind made the reply blandly, as if he had simply misunderstood.

George returned to his book. The imperfect with the perfect of another verb expresses the future perfect: *Zaid will have written.* (Another glass was smashed, this time in a subdued way. A human voice could be heard, though not understood.) When it is an independent verb, the subject is in the nominative and the complement in the accusative: *The apostle will be a witness against you.*

"Listen," Rosalind said with the doomsday hiss of a wife who at night smells gas. He listened, hearing nothing. Then Mrs. Irva began to scream.

George immediately hoped that the woman was joking. The noises she made might have meant anything: fear, joy, anger, exuberance. They might have been produced mechanically, by the rhythmic friction of a huge and useful machine. It seemed likely that they would stop.

"What are you going to do?" Rosalind asked him. She had risen and was standing close to him, giving off an oppressive aroma of concern.

"Do?"

"Is there anyone we could get?"

Their janitor, a slender, blue-jawed Pole, was in charge of three other houses and a grammar school, and made his visitations furtively, around dawn and midnight. Their landlady, a grim Jewish widow, lived across the Park, at a more acceptable address. Their only neighbor other than the Irvas was a young Chinese student in a room at the back of the building, behind the Chandlers' bedroom. His examinations over, he had inked, in a beautiful black calligraphy, an Ohio forwarding address onto the wall above his mailbox, and left.

"No, Karl! Decency!" Mrs. Irva shouted. Her voice, mingled with confused tumbling effects, had lost its early brilliance. Now hoarse, now shrill, her mouthings were frantic. "No, no, no, no, please God no!"

"He's killing her, George. George, what *are you doing?*"

"Doing?"

"Must *I* call the police?" She glared at him with an icy contempt that her good nature melted in seconds. She went to the wall and leaned against it gracefully, her mouth wide open. "They're turning on the faucet," she whispered.

Bolder, George asked, "Should we interfere?"

"Wait. They're so quiet now."

"They—"

"Sh-h-h!"

George said, "She's dead, honey. He's washing the blood off his hands." Even in these taut circumstances, he could not resist kidding her. In her excitement she fell right in with it.

"He has, hasn't he?" she agreed. Then, seeing his smile, she said, "You don't think he has."

He squeezed her soft forearm kindly.

"George, he really has killed her," Rosalind said. "That's why there's no noise. Break in!"

"Stop and think, honey. How do you know they're not—?"

Her eyes widened as the thought dawned on her. "Are there really people like that?" She was confused; the room beyond the wall was silent; it seemed to George that he had brought the incident to a conclusion.

"Help, please help," Mrs. Irva called, rather calmly. Evidently this enraged her attacker, for in a moment she screamed with an intensity that choked her, as a baby at the height of a tantrum will nearly strangle.

The noise, so irrational, such a poor reward for his patience, infuriated George. With precipitous irritation he opened his door and stepped into the square of uncarpeted boards that served as an entrance hall to the three apartments. Standing there in its center, he seemed to see himself across a great span of time, as if he were an old man recalling a youthful exploit, recounting his finest hour. Fearless and lucid, he rapped his knuckles below the tacked card: "Mr. and Mrs. Karl Irva." He sang out, "Everybody all right in there?"

"Be careful," Rosalind pleaded, at the same time resting her hands on his back, threatening a shove. He turned to rebuke her and was offended to discover that, because of his crouching and her tiptoeing, her eyes were inches higher than his.

"Do you want to run in yourself?" he snapped and, without thinking, turned the knob of the Irvas' door. It had not been locked.

He swung the door in timidly, gaining an upright slice of an American interior: dimly figured carpet, a slice of purple chair, a straw wastebasket beneath a television set seen sidewise, a bamboo lamp, a propped-up photograph, ochre wall, bad green ceiling. Nothing reflected irregularity. From the large unseen portion of the room, Mrs. Irva called, "Go away—he has a knife!" At the sound of her voice George slammed the door shut instinctively, keeping his hand on the knob, as if the door were his shield.

"We must help her," Rosalind insisted.

"Get off my back," he said.

"Lord," Mrs. Irva moaned. George pushed open the

door again, far enough to see one trace of disorder—an undershirt on a sofa arm. "Stay out!" the unseen woman called. "He has a knife." Again he closed the door.

A voice unmistakably Mr. Irva's asked without inflection, "Who have you fetched?" No answer was made. George was relieved. Though he had not seen Mrs. Irva, she might have supposed who he was. Footsteps unexpectedly thumped toward them, and the young couple fled to their own apartment, Rosalind skinning her husband's arm as she shut and bolted their door.

Here George, in telling the story, would hold his elbow outward and with the stiffened fingers of his other hand indicate precisely how the metal edge of the lock projection caught the flat area on the side of his forearm and scraped the skin blue, right through his shirt—ripped the shirt, too. A four-dollar shirt. His emphasis on this detail was clearly for his wife's benefit, but she failed to consider herself chided, and her wide triangular face expressed only a pretty anxiety to have the narrative continue. Rosalind, the daughter of a scholar-poet who had gone to the Southwest as an act of renunciation and renewal, was in turn quite unself-conscious about her mind. Her gaps in judgment were startling. Over her Doric figure she wore dresses printed with violins, half-notes, clef signatures, and busts of Beethoven. She mispronounced even simple names—Sart-er, Hāzlitt, Maugh-hum. In time, anticipating George's hurried, embarrassed correction, she came to pause and smile considerately at company before blundering. "And what I liked best were some pink fish and stick figures by a wonderful painter called, Klēē?" Yet she remembered some things excellently: shops and streets, characters in novels she had enjoyed, infielders, minor movie actors. When George's arm-scraping demonstration was completed, she would say, "One of the policemen who finally came looked just like John Ireland. Only younger, and not so nice."

It had been Rosalind who had called them; George was in the bathroom dabbing boric acid on his wound. Following the instructions on page one of the telephone directory, she dialed zero and said, "I want a policeman."

The operator, mistaking Rosalind for a teen-ager, asked, "You're sure now, honey?" She was always being called "honey."

"I really do."

The two cops who came twelve minutes later were young, and plainly in process of being wised up. They stood frowning in the Chandlers' doorway, shoulder to shoulder, just two decent ex-M.P.s trying to make an honest buck in a rotten world. First off, their eyes were very interested in the third finger of Rosalind's left hand. As soon as the one that looked a little like John Ireland saw the glint of gold there, he turned his attention to George, but the other one kept at it, trying to get his eyes around the ring, under it, giving it the acid bath. His eyes, which had the pale crystalline irises of the very dumb, narrowed cannily, and he shifted them to Rosalind's face.

"We were given this apartment number," John said.

He looked at a slip of paper and read each figure separately, "Five, four, A."

"That door there," George said, unnecessarily pointing over the cop's shoulder. He was frightened; his hand shook badly. The cops took this in. "We heard a glass break about two hours ago, around eight o'clock."

"It's nine-oh-five now," the other cop said, looking at his wristwatch.

"It seems later," Rosalind said. The eyes of both policemen focused on her lips. The suspicious one grimaced with the effort of letting nothing about her voice—light, cultured, slower than the voices of most tarts—escape him.

George took courage from his wife's reminder that he had been given bad service. With new authority he described the sounds and screams they had heard. "There's been some rumpus after we called you, but for the last six minutes or so there's been no noise. We would have heard if there had been—these walls are so goddam thin." He smiled slightly, to go with the swearing, but it won him no friends.

The other cop wrote scrunchily in a little pad. "Six minutes or *so*," he muttered. George had no idea why he had said six minutes instead of five. It did sound fishy. "Since you called us, you stayed in your room?"

"We didn't want to enrage him," George said.

John Ireland, his needle nose in the air, rapped delicately on the Irvas' door. Getting no answer, he toed it open. They all followed him in. The room was empty. One chair was overturned. Flakes and shards of glass glittered on the carpet. The disorder in the room was less than it should have been; the Chandlers were disappointed and shamed.

Yet now, when they seemed to themselves most vulnerable, the policemen failed to bully them. John Ireland undid the little snap on his holster. The other one said, "Blood on the sofa arm." Moving into the kitchenette, he said, in a murmur that carried, "Strings of blood in the sink."

Strings of blood! "Her cries became more and more frantic," George said.

John Ireland stuck his head out of a window.

The other cop asked, "Miss, is there a phone in here?"

"We never hear it ring," Rosalind said.

"We have a phone in our apartment," George told them. He was eager to succeed in his new role of cops' ally. That they all faced a common enemy was clear now. Perhaps Irva was behind the shower curtain, or stood outside the window, on the tiny concrete balcony, advertised as "terrace," which the Chandlers could see when they risked stepping out onto their own. A sense of danger spread through the room like iodine in water. John Ireland moved quickly away from the window. The other cop came in from the kitchen. The three men gathered around the door, waiting, with a strained courtesy, for Rosalind to go first.

She stepped into the little hall and screamed; astounded, George leaped and embraced her from behind. The cops came after. On the first landing of the stairs going up to the next floor, at the level of their heads, Mrs. Irva crouched on all fours, staring at them, in her eyes an obscure and watery emotion. Her right forearm was solidly red with blood. You forget how bright blood is. The right side of her slip was torn, exposing one breast. She said nothing.

What had happened, the Chandlers later decided, was that after Mr. Irva left (they wondered in retrospect if a door hadn't slammed), Mrs. Irva, afraid, had run up the stairs and then, feeling weak, or curious about the conversations downstairs, had begun to crawl down again. There was a lot this didn't explain. Why should she have left the room *after* her husband had gone? On the other hand, if he had chased her up the stairs, why wasn't he still up there with her? One cop had gone up and looked and found nothing. Perhaps Irva had been up there when the police arrived and had sneaked down when they were all in his apartment. He could even have taken the elevator down, though this seemed a cool thing to do. The elevator in the building was self-service, and if anybody on a lower floor had rung, the elevator, with the villain in it, would have stopped to let him on. Yet weren't the walls thin enough for them to have heard Mr. Irva's footsteps?

Mrs. Irva shed no light. She looked so sunken no one pressed her for information. The cops led her into the Chandlers' apartment and had her lie on the odorous sofa that had come with the place. John told Rosalind to bring two towels from the bathroom and asked George if there was any hard liquor around. When Rosalind brought the towels (guest towels, George saw), John tore one lengthwise to make a tourniquet. The Chandlers drank seldom, being both thrifty and health-minded, but they did have some sherry in the kitchen cabinet, behind a loaf of Pepperidge Farm bread. George poured some into a tumbler and handed it timidly to Mrs. Irva, by now rather dapper in her tourniquet. Her broken slip strap had been knotted. She politely took a sip and said "Fine," though she drank no more. Rosalind brought in a yellow blanket from the bedroom. She spread it over Mrs. Irva, then went into the kitchen and began to heat water.

"What are you doing?" George asked her.

"He told me to make coffee," she said, nodding toward the cop who did not look like any movie star.

The one who did came and stood by George; having this blue uniform brush against him made George feel arrested. "Takes all types," he muttered uneasily.

"Buddy, this is nothing," the policeman answered. "This is tame. Stuff worse than this happens every minute in this city."

George began to like him. "I believe it," he said. "Hell, I was in the subway two weeks ago and a young kid took a swing at me."

John shook his head. "Buddy, that's nothing compared to what I see every day. Every day of the week."

The ambulance came before the coffee water boiled. Two Negroes were admitted. One was dressed in crisp white and carried a folded stretcher, which he unravelled with a conjurer's zest. The other, taller, logier, and perhaps recently from the South, wore a maroon sports jacket over the thin coat of his uniform. They eased Mrs. Irva into the stretcher; she was passive, but her mouth worked with fright when she felt herself being lifted. "Eeasy theah," the tall bearer said. The ambulance men had noticed on the way up that the elevator was too small for the stretcher; they had to walk down four flights, the front one holding the handles at shoulder height.

The policemen lingered a moment in the elevator, facing the Chandlers, who hung together in the doorway like the host couple after a shindig. "O.K.," John said threateningly. The elevator door sucked shut, and the cops dropped from view.

From their window George and Rosalind could see the pavement, dotted with foreshortened spectators. These human beings made an aisle down which the four public servants with their burden passed. Mrs. Irva, a yellow rectangle from five stories up, was inserted into the gray rectangle of the ambulance. The policemen got into their green and white and black Ford, and the two vehicles pulled away from the curb precisely together, like night-club dancers. The ambulance moaned irritably and didn't begin to wail until it was down the block, out of sight.

George tried to return to his Arabic, but his wife was too excited, and they stayed awake until one o'clock, twisting and talking in bed. For the sixth time Rosalind regretted that she had not seen the one policeman tie Mrs. Irva's slip strap. Again George objected that most likely she tied it herself.

"With her arm cut to the bone?"

"It wasn't cut to the bone, honey. It was just a nick."

She pounded her pillow and dropped her head into it. "I know he did it. That would have been just like him. The one with the blunt nose was much sweeter."

"After the way he looked at you at the door? Didn't you see him look at your wedding ring?"

"At least he paid some attention to me. The other one was in love with *you*." Rosalind saw homosexuals everywhere.

Next morning they could hear Mrs. Irva in her apartment, vacuuming. Several days later, George went down in the elevator with her. He asked her how she was feeling. No bandage showed; she was wearing long sleeves.

She beamed. "Very decent. And how's yourself and your nice wife?"

"All right," George said, nettled to have his question taken as a pleasantry. He prodded her with "You got home all right?"

"Oh, yes," she said. "They were such nice men."

George didn't understand. The policemen? The doctors at the hospital? The fourth, the third, the second floors passed them in silence.

"My husband—" Mrs. Irva began. They had reached the ground floor; the door drew open.

"What about your husband?"

"Yes, he doesn't blame you and your wife in the slightest," she said, and then smiled as if she had just uttered a gracious invitation. And she hadn't even mentioned his blanket.

George missed that yellow blanket. For him, May nights in New York were chilly. He was here looking for a job that would take him to Arabia or some other Moslem place. The quest led him into the disillusioned section of town between the West Forties and the Village, into the Wall Street area, into the sour waiting rooms of oil companies, export outfits, shippers, banks with overseas branches. Receptionists were impolite. Personnel men, pressing their fingertips together to hide the tremor, were tired and frightened by the new science of employment. George puzzled them. There was no space on their forms where Arabophilia could be entered.

It *was* hard to coördinate this passion for the desert with George's plump, sulky face and married personality. He seldom explained. But late in an evening spent with friends he might blurt out a description of how the Danakil fish for trocas in the Red Sea. "It's fantastic. They walk around on these reefs and dip their whole bodies under water whenever they see one of these big snails. Then the wind coming down from Egypt dries them so their entire bodies are white with salt. The stuff they're walking on is brittle, and when it breaks through it scrapes the skin off their legs. Then poisonous jellyfish sting them, so as they move along they sing at the top of their lungs to scare them away. You can smell one of these fishing boats six miles away on account of the rotting snails in the hold. At night, they sleep on these little boats with millions of black flies getting into their food. Fifty miles away is the Arabian coast with nothing on it but pirates. And here are these guys singing to keep the poisonous jellyfish away. You wonder—I know what you're thinking." Nobody knew what he was thinking, but an expression on one of the faces turned toward him would make him think he was making a fool of himself.

He might, at another time, lambaste modern housing —the plains outside of Phoenix covered with ugly pas-

tel boxes arranged on phony curving streets, the super-
markets, the widening highways, the land going under
all over. This was more like George; he advanced his
intellect negatively, by extending his contempt. All
movies were lousy, all politicians were crooked, public
education in America was the world's worst, most novels were a waste of time, everybody on television was
out for your money. He had pieced together his education out of his parents' fears and the sly hints of
half-baked instructors. George was proud of what he
knew; he had not discovered that at the "good" col-
leges (he was eager to admit that his own college had
been no good) one liked everything—Western movies, corny music, trashy books, crooked politicos, silly
girls—and reserved distaste for great men.

A friend looking through the Chandlers' library
(mostly old political-science textbooks, and paperback
mysteries, which Rosalind chain-read) might pull
down, because it alone suggested Arabia, *Hashish*, by
Henri de Monfreid, and find underlined—the under-
lining, thick soft pencil, was unmistakably George—
the sentence "The heat of the day breathed out from
the walls and ground like an immense sigh of relief."
But facing a preoccupied executive across a glass-
topped desk, George could only say, with a compro-
mising snicker, "I guess it *is* silly, but ever since I was
a kid I've been fascinated by those places."

"No, I don't think it's silly," would be the answer.

A month after the Irvas' fight, Rosalind stood outside their door and greeted George at his homecoming
with, "The most wonderful thing has happened!"

"I bet." He was coming up the stairs; a woman who lived on the third floor had stepped into the elevator with him, and since the machine tended to return to the ground floor after one stop, he had got out with her and walked up two flights. His day had been frustrating. The most promising possibility, working with the United States delegation to a trade fair in Basra, appeared to have fallen through. It had taken him three quarters of an hour to see Mr. Guerin again, and then he was told nothing but that funds were limited. He was so depressed that he had gone into a 38¢ movie, but it was something old with Barbara Stanwyck and so bad he had to leave, feeling sick. In a luncheonette on East Thirty-third Street he was charged $1.10 for a turkey sandwich, a glass of milk, and a cup of coffee. When he gave the cashier a five-dollar bill, she insisted that he also produce a dime and three pennies for tax, and then dealt the four dollars change not into his waiting hand but, rudely, onto the counter. As if he were covered with germs. On his way home, the mobs choking the subways, clustering at intersections, dodging, wisecracking, seemed one huge contamination. It was his eleventh week of hunting. Rosalind's department-store job, which was for only six hours a day now that the Easter rush had subsided, did not quite take care of rent and food. The Chandlers were eating into their savings at the rate of fifty dollars a month.

Rosalind stood between him and their door. This annoyed George; he was tired. "Wait," Rosalind said. Holding up a palm, she prolonged her own delight. "Have you seen either of the Irvas lately? Think."

"I never see *him*. Once in a while Mrs. and I get

caught in the elevator together." After his first conversation, he had not tried to sound Mrs. Irva out on
the incident, and there seemed to be so little connection between the crazed and naked sufferer of that
night and this compact little woman, with her hair going white in stripes and black buttons down the front
of her blouse and an orange mouth painted up over
the natural edge of her upper lip, that it was easy for
George to discuss with her the weather and the poor
way the building was run, as if they had nothing more
important between them.

"What *is* this routine?" George asked after Rosalind
had stood silent for a moment, on her face this inane
gaiety.

"Behold, effendi," she said, opening the door.

Inside the room George saw flowers everywhere,
white, pink, yellow, tall flowers, motionless, in vases,
pitchers, and wastebaskets, lying in bundles on tables
and chairs and on the floor. George never knew the
names of flowers, but these were a public sort, big and
hardy. Benevolence breathed from their long, igno-
rant, complex faces. The air in the room had a flower-
shop coolness.

"They came in a station wagon. Mrs. Irva said they
were used to decorate a banquet last night, and the man
in charge said the chef should have them. Mr. Irva
thought it would be nice to give them to us. To show
that everything was right between our families, Mrs.
Irva said."

George was puzzled, stopped. His mind, swept clean
of assertion, knew nothing but the flowers; they

poured through his eyes. Later, in the stink and strangeness of Basra, whenever the homesick couple tried to recall America, the image that first and most vividly came to George was that of those massed idiot beauties.

A Trillion Feet of Gas

OLD MAN FRAELICH, THE INSTANT THEY ENTERED HIS room, rose in his pearl-pale suit and intoned flatulently, "John, let's you and I go downstairs."

Another man, in black, got to his feet.

"That would be rude," Mrs. Fraelich stated, more as a simple fact than a reprimand, though it might have been her influence—it was hard to guess how much power she had over her husband—that induced Fraelich to shake hands with his three young guests, listening to their names and gazing above their heads while his inflated pink hand, apparently cut off from his brain and acting on its own decent instincts, floated forward from his vest. Under those averted eyes Luke felt like a rich pastry mistakenly offered to an ill man. Had Fraelich forgotten the several times they had met before?

Kathy, introducing her guests to her father-in-law with the angular exaggerations of a girl whose beauty is her sole defense, also implied they were strangers. "Father, this is Elizabeth Forrest, and Luther Forrest."

"You remember Luke from school," Tim told him.

"Of course I have," Fraelich said evenly, changing his son's verb and tilting back his head, as if into a pillow, so that he looked sicker than ever; his complexion had the sheen of a skin sweating out a fever. Luke suddenly got the idea that Liz's being pregnant had offended him.

"And Mr. Boyce-King from England," Kathy continued.

"Just King," Donald corrected, blushing quickly. "Don King. *Bryce* is the middle name."

"*Not* a hyphen!" Kathy cried, insisting, in the midst of her in-laws and her husband's friends, on her right to be natural and gay. Fatigue added to her lean charm all the romantic suggestions of exhaustion. Luke had been told she was undergoing analysis. "Pardon *me*. I only heard your name once over the phone."

"It's awfully good of you to have me," Donald said mechanically.

"He looks like a hyphen person, doesn't he?" Liz said, helping the other girl out, and unwittingly reflecting the ironic discussions she and Luke had had about their English guest in the few hours since Monday when Donald had not been with them. "I think it's his eyebrows."

In the background Mrs. Fraelich had got to her feet, swinging her arms in boredom or exasperation. As she did so, the décolletage of her dress—a tube of soft blue cloth with big holes cut for the throat and arms, as in old copies of *Vanity Fair*—wandered alarmingly over her gaunt, freckled chest. She offered her second fact to the group. "Here is Mr. Born."

For the first time Fraelich showed animation. "Yes," he announced, and his voice ballooned, "we can't forget John Born." The man in black, stout but solid, gave each of the young people a firm handshake and an identical expression of pleasure. His suit and mustache were identically dark. Luke was delighted that Donald was meeting, even wordlessly, an authentic specimen of the Manhattan rich. Fraelich was rich but scarcely authentic.

The old people scattered to other quarters of the duplex, and the young people were left alone with the bulwark-style leather furniture, Mrs. Fraelich's Japanese water colors, and the parabolic sub-ceiling suspended and glowing *à la* restaurant.

"Please forgive the hyphen; it's a fantasy of mine that all Englishmen have double names," Kathy said to Donald, who, with the abrupt ease of the British, was examining, his head atilt, the spines of the books on the shelves.

"Not at all. I enjoyed it."

The smug inappropriateness of the remark tipped them into a difficult silence. An awkward evening seemed foreshadowed. Most of the strands of acquaintance between the five were tenuous. Luke had known Tim at college, and had met Donald in England, and the two wives were, considering the slightness of their acquaintance, fond of each other. They made the best of it, chatting and sipping yellow drinks just like grownups. Luke kept wanting to suggest that they play Monopoly. Fraelich must have a set, and it would be a good American game for Donald to learn. Dinner evidently would be quite late. A new factor, hunger, was added to the nervous unrest in Luke's stomach.

He talked to Tim of common friends. Neither had heard anything from Irv. Preston Wentworth, Tim thought, was on the West Coast. Leo Bailley *had* been in town. It was strange how completely you could lose sight of men you saw every day in college. Our generation just doesn't write letters, Luke offered.

Donald said he thought that Americans phoned everywhere, or had little boys in wingèd boots carrying singing messages.

Kathy asked Liz how she felt. Liz said she felt just the same, but clumsier; that it was surprising how much you felt like your old self; and that she was looking forward to the contented-cow stage mentioned in the motherhood books. Donald laughed at motherhood books. Luke saw Kathy send Liz, by wingèd facial expression, a message that probably read, "We're thinking about babies, too, but Timothy . . ." "How nice or sad," Liz's face sent back. Donald, trapped near the intersection of these baby-looks, experienced another flash of discomfiture and blushed stuffily. He had the oval slant eyes and full-fleshed lips of the British intellectual, and the raw sloping forehead.

Tim Fraelich, sensing that his three guests had been together so much that in relation to each other they were speechless, assumed the role of topic starter. He mentioned the Olympic Games. Luke joined in gratefully. Since his interceding with, "You remember Luke from school," Luke loved Tim, his slow considerate mind and his ugly laborer's face. The blessing of money, in combination with modest endowments otherwise, had made Tim very gentle. In the Areté Club—he had been president when Luke was a sophomore—he had hated that anyone must be blackballed, whereas Luke, who knew that his own election had been close, proudly and recklessly wielded the veto.

The Olympic discussion died soon. Luke couldn't think of any stars except Perry O'Brien, and the vaulting preacher Richards, and the young Negro—what was his name?—who jumped seven feet.

Swift and strong Americans, Donald said, appeared on the scene like waves of industrial produce.

But it was the Commonwealth, they hastened to assure him, that demolished the four-minute mile. The Forrests, their year in Oxford, had lived a block away from the Iffley track, where Bannister had run the first one. Donald had been at Oxford at the time but hadn't bothered to attend the meet. He seemed to feel a certain distinction lay in this.

Tim asked his English guest what he had seen of New York so far—if he had seen such-and-such an interesting place. Lamentably, nothing Tim named had Donald seen. The Forrests had been poor guides, though they had worked hard. Preceded by a radiogram, Donald had arrived on a Dutch liner, penniless and in the show-me mood of a cultural delegation. With the politico-literary precocity of Oxford youth, he had already been published in one of the British liberal weeklies, and he seemed to imagine that visiting the transatlantic land mass would constitute a scoop, Mrs. Trollope alone preceding him. Cruelly harried by their sense of official responsibility, the Forrests, after displaying to him their own selves—typical of the rising generation, he with a job in media and she with Scandinavian tastes, favoring natural wood and natural childbirth—had arranged parties and suppers where the allegorical figures of College Student, Unwed Secretary, Struggling Cubist, Poet-Claustrophobe, Luminous Jewess, Actor, Comer, Intellectual Catholic, and Corporation Lawyer filed across the stage of their visitor's preconceptions. Luke described in sociological detail his childhood in a small Ohio town, and Liz contributed what she knew of the caste system in Massachusetts. Donald, though polite, was rarely moved. Luke and Liz whispered guiltily in bed at night if, when the guests were gone, Donald did not withdraw his notebook from his coat pocket and take it to the sofa with a pencil and his final drink of the day. He drank steadily and soberly. In the daytime, Liz, saying that pregnant women should walk lots anyway, took Donald hunting for useful sights. She led him through Chinatown, the Village, Wall Street, the kosher districts, and at Luke's evening homecoming complained, as Donald sat sipping joylessly, his silence giving assent, that everything is just buildings and cars, that she felt so sorry for Donald, being stuck with them.

Their guest claimed he did plan to leave. He wanted to see the "Southland," and especially "your plains." But no trip could begin until a money order arrived from somewhere—Canada, they thought he said. The Forrests had nicknamed it "the packet from France." In the close company the three kept, the joke had come into the open. For several breakfasts, Luke had asked,

"The packet from France arrive?" Liz, noting Donald's diminishing response, warned her husband that he gave the impression of hinting. Luke said it wasn't a hint, it was a pleasantry, and anyway, it didn't look to him as if Donald was very sensitive to hints or indeed anything.

It was true, the Englishman's calm—so cheering in Oxford, so strong that, even meeting him on High Street, against a background of steelworkers on bicycles and whey-faced bus queues, you smelled pipe smoke, and felt the safety of his room in Magdalen, with the old novels in many thin volumes and the window giving onto the deer park and the drab London magazines stacked like dolls' newspapers on the mantel—in America had become a maddening quiescence, as if the thicker sunlight of this more southern country were a physical weight on his limbs. He had protested the bother of being included in this dinner engagement, but he had not suggested, as they had hoped, that he could manage a night on his own.

"No," he was saying to Tim, "they haven't taken me to Louie's. You say it's an interesting place. Does it have lots of ethos? You Americans are always talking about ethos. Margaret Mead is sort of your White Goddess over here, isn't she?"

"Mamie is," Kathy suddenly said, thrusting her fingers into the hair at her temples and laughing when the others did.

Donald said that once again the American people had proven themselves idiots in the eyes of the world. Luke said it would be a different story in 1960. "Wait till sixty, wait till sixty," Donald said. "That's all you people think about. The 1960 model of Plymouth car; the population will be two billion in 1960. You're in love with the future." He touched, in an unconscious gesture, the breast of his coat, to make sure the stiffness of the notebook was there. Luke smiled and saw them all through Donald's eyes: the mild, homely heir, his fretful, leggy wife, Liz with her half-formed baby, Luke himself with his half-baked success—pale, pale. Poor Americans, these, for the *New Statesman & Nation*. What Donald couldn't see that Luke could was how well he, Donald, his sensible English shoes cracked and his wool clothes faded, blended into their pastel frieze.

The man introduced to them as Mr. Born walked into the room. "Looks like Ah'll be getting a ride," he said to Tim. "With your father and mother." His voice, as Luke had expected, was rich and grainy, but the accent forced a slight revision of his first idea of the man. He was Southern. In the black suit, Born's body, solid as a barrel, stood out with peculiar force against the linen-covered wall, where Mrs. Fraelich's Japanese prints made patches of vague color.

"Would you like a Scotch-and-water, John?" Tim asked. "Or cognac?" Mr. Born shook his massive head —severed from his body, it might have weighed forty pounds—and held up his square, exquisitely clean hand to halt all liquor traffic. In the other he gripped a heavy cigar, freshly lighted.

"We've been chewing over the election," Tim said.

"You desahd who won it?"

The young people made a fragile noise of laughter.

"We've been deciding who should have won it," Donald said, cross spots appearing on his cheekbones and forehead.

"Yeass," Mr. Born said, simultaneous with the hissing of the cushions as he settled into a leather armchair. "There was never any doubt about the way it would go in Texas. The betting in Houston wasn't on *who*— his lips pushed forward on the prolonged "who"— would get it but at what *taam* the other man would con*cede*." He rotated the cigar a half-circle, so the burning end was toward himself. "A lot of money was lost in Houston while Adlai was making that speech so good. They thought, you see, it would be *soon*er."

"How did you do?" Donald asked tactlessly, as if this were an exhibit they had arranged for him.

"Noo." The Texan scratched his ear fastidiously and beamed. "I had no money on it."

"What *is* the situation out there? Politically? One reads the Democrats are in bad shape," Donald said.

The broad healthy face bunched as he pleasantly studied the boy. "What they say, Lyndon didn't show up too good at the convention. We aren't all that proud of him. As I heard it expressed, the feeling was, let those two run and get killed and get rid of 'em that way. That's the way I've heard it expressed: Run those two, and let 'em get killed."

"Really!" Kathy exclaimed. Then, surprised at herself, she bit her lower lip coquettishly and crossed her legs, calling attention to them. Luke liked her legs because above the lean and urban ankles the calves swelled to a country plumpness.

"The American scramble," Donald murmured.

Luke, afraid Mr. Born would feel hostility in the air,

asked why the South hadn't pushed someone like Gore instead of Kennedy.

"Gore's not *pop*ular. The answer's very simple: The South doesn't have anyone big enough. 'Cept Lyndon. And he's sick. Heart attack. No, they're in a bad way down there. They have the leaders of both houses, and they're in a bad way."

"Wouldn't there be a certain amount of anti-Catholic sentiment stirred up if Kennedy were to run?" Tim asked. His mother, for a period in her youth, had been a convert to the Church.

Mr. Born puffed his cigar and squinted at his friend's son through the smoke. "I think we've outgrown that. I think we've outgrown that."

The rough bulge of Donald's forehead shone scarlet. He blurted, "You're pleased with the way things went?"

"Well. I voted for Aahk. Not particularly proud of it, though. Not particularly proud of it. He vetoed our gas bill." Everyone laughed, for no clear reason. "If he had it to do over again, he wouldn't *do* it."

"You think so?" Donald asked.

"I know it for a *faact*. He's said so. He wants the bill. And Adlai, he wouldn't promise if he got in he wouldn't try to get the Lands back to Washington. So we voted Aahk in; he was the best we could get."

Donald pointed at him gingerly. "You, of course, don't want the Tidelands to revert to the federal government."

"They *can't*. There won't be any gas. It's off twelve per cent from last year now, for the *needs*. You see— Are you all interested in this?"

The group nodded hastily.

"I have a trillion feet of gas. It's down there. In the ground. It's not gone to go away. Now, I made a contract to sell that gas at eighteen cents in Chicago. In the city of Chicago there are maybe twelve thousand meters now that don't have adequate supply. I wanted to pipe it up, from Texas. That was two years ago. They won't let me do it. I've been in Washington, D.C., for most of those two years, trying to see a bill passed that'll let me *do* it." He released some smoke and smiled. Washington, the implication was, had agreed with him.

Donald asked why they wouldn't let him do it. Mr. Born explained in detail—clearly and kindly, and even got to his feet to explain—federal agencies, state commissions, wellhead quotas, costs of distillate, dry holes ("They don't allow you for drah holes *after;* the ones up *to,* okay, but then they don't recognize 'em."), and the Socialist color of thinking in Washington. On and on it went, a beautiful composition, vowel upon vowel, occasional emphasis striking like an oboe into a passage of cellos. The coda came too soon: "But the point, the point is this: If they *do* pass it, then fine. I'm contracted out; I'm willing to stick by it. But if they *don't* —if they don't, then I sell it for more *inside Texas.* That's how demand is gone up."

Luke realized with delight that here, a yard from his eyes, walked and talked a bugaboo—a Tidelands lobbyist, a States' Righter, a purchaser of Congressmen, a pillar of reaction. And what had he proved to be, this stout man holding his huge head forward from his spine, bisonlike? A companion all simplicity and courtesy, bearing without complaint—and all for the sake, it seemed, of these young people—the unthinkable burden of a trillion feet of gas. Luke could not remember the reasons for governmental control of big business any better than he could recall when drunk the defects of his own personality. With a gentle three-finger grip on his cigar, Mr. Born settled back into the armchair, the viewpoints alternative to his hanging vaporized in the air around him, a flattering haze.

The next minute Mr. and Mrs. Fraelich came and took John Born away, though not before old man Fraelich, his gray bulbous voice droning anxiously, exuded every fact he knew about the natural-gas industry. Mr. Born listened politely, tilting his stogie this way and that. The possibility occurred to Luke that, as Mr. Born owned a trillion feet of gas, Mr. Fraelich owned John Born.

"He's really a hell of a nice guy," Tim said when the older people had gone.

"Oh, he was wonderful!" Liz said. "The way he stood there, so big in his black suit—" She encircled an area with her arms and, without thinking, thrust out her stomach.

Kathy asked, "Did he mean a trillion feet of gas in the pipe?"

"No, no, you fluff," Tim said, giving her a bullying hug that jarred Luke. "*Cubic* feet."

"That still doesn't mean anything to me," Liz said. "Can't you compress gas?"

"Where does he keep it?" Kathy asked. "I mean have it."

"In the ground," Luke said. "Weren't you listening?"

"Gas like you burn?"

"A trillion," Donald said, tentatively sarcastic. "I don't even know how many ciphers are in it."

"Twelve in America," Luke said. "In Britain, more. Eighteen."

"You Americans are so good at figgers. Yankee ingenuity."

"Watch it, Boyce-King. If you British don't learn how to say 'figures' we'll pipe that gas under your island and make it a satellite."

Though no one else laughed, Luke himself did, at the picture of England as a red pie plate skimming through space, fragments chipping off until nothing remained but the dome of St. Paul's. And, after they had sat down to dinner, he continued to be quite funny, frequently at the expense of "Boyce-King." He felt back in college, full of novel education and undulled ambition. Kathy Fraelich laughed until her hand shook over the soup. It was good to know he could still make people laugh. ". . . but the *great* movies are the ones where an idol teeters, you know, all grinning and bug-eyed—" he wobbled rigidly in his chair and then with horrible slow menace fell forward, breaking off the act just as his nose touched the rim of the water glass—"and then crumbles all over the screaming worshippers. They don't make scenes like that in British movies. They save their idols and pawn them off as Druid shrines. Or else scratch 'Wellington' across the front. Ah, you're a canny race, Boyce-King."

After dinner they watched two television plays, which Luke ingeniously defended as fine art at every turn of the action, Donald squirming and blinking and the others not even listening but attending to the screen. Liz loved TV. The young Fraelichs nuzzled together in one fat chair. The black-and-white figures —Luke said "figgers"—were outlined on Fraelich's costly color set with rainbows.

Luke, at the door, thanked their hosts enthusiastically for the excellent meal, the educational company, the iridescent dramas. The two couples expanded the last goodbye with a discussion of where to live eventually. They decided, while Donald nodded and chuckled uneasily on the fringe of the exchange, that nothing was as important as the children feeling secure in a place.

In the taxi, Luke, sorry that in the end Donald had seemed an extra party, said to him, "Well, we've shown you the Texas Billionaire. You've gazed into the heart of a great nation."

"Did you notice his hands?" Liz asked. "They were really beautiful." She was in a nice, tranquil mood.

"It was extraordinary," Donald said, squeezed in the middle and uncertain where his arms should go, "the way he held you all, with his consistently selfish reasoning."

Luke put his arm on the back of the seat, including his visitor in a non-tactile embrace and touching Liz's neck with his fingers. The packet from France, he reckoned, was on the way. The head of the cabby jerked as he tried to make out his passengers in the rearview mirror. "You're afraid," Luke said loudly, "of our hideous vigor."

Incest

"I WAS IN A MOVIE HOUSE, FAIRLY PLUSH, IN A SORT OF mezzanine, or balcony. It was a wide screen. On it there were tall people—it seemed to be at a dance or at least *function*—talking and bending toward each other gracefully, in that misty technicolor Japanese pictures have. I *knew* that this was the movie version of *Remembrance of Things Past*. I had the impression sitting there that I had been looking forward to it for a long time, and I felt slightly guilty at not being home, you know. There was a girl sitting down one row, catty-corner from me. She had a small head with a thin, rather touching neck, like Moira Lengel, but it wasn't her, or anyone we know. At any rate there was this feeling of great affection toward her, and it seemed, in the light of the movie—the movie was taking place entirely in a bright yellow ballroom, so the faces of the audience were clear—it seemed somehow that the entire chance to make my life good was wrapped up in this girl, who was strange to me. Then she was in the seat beside me, and I was giving her a back rub."

"*Uh*-oh," his wife said, pausing in her stooping. She was grazing the carpet, picking up the toys, cards, matches, and spoons scattered by their daughter Jane, a year and seven months old. Big Jane, as she had dreaded being called when they named the child, held quite still to catch what next he had to tell. Lee had begun the recitation ironically, to register his irritation with her for asking him, her own day had been so dull and wearing, to talk, to tell her of *his* day. Nothing interested him less than his own day, done. It made his jaws ache, as with a smothered yawn, to consider framing one sentence about it. So, part desperation, part discipline, he had begun the account of the dream he had been careful to keep from her at breakfast. He protected his wife here, at the place where he recalled feeling his hands leave the lean girl's comforted shoulder blades and travel thoughtfully around the cool, strait, faintly ridged sides of the rib case to the always surprising boon in front—sensations momentarily more vivid in the nerves of his fingers than the immediate texture of the bamboo chair he occupied.

"Through the blouse."

"Good," she said. "Good for you both."

Jane appeared so saucy saying this he was emboldened to add a true detail: "I think I did undo her bra strap. By pinching through the cloth." To judge by his wife's expression—tense for him, as if he were bragging before company—the addition was a mistake. He hastened on. "Then we were standing in back of the seats, behind one of those walls that comes up to your chest, and I was being introduced to her father. I had the impression he was a doctor. He was rather pleasant, really: gray hair, and a firm grip. He seemed cordial, and I had a competent feeling, as if I couldn't help making a good impression. But behind this encounter—with the girl standing off to one side—there was the sadness of the movie itself continuing on the screen; the music soared; Proust's face was shown— a very young face—with the eyelids closed, and this shimmered and spun and turned into a slow pink vortex that then solidified into a huge motionless rose, filling the whole screen. And I thought, *Now I know how the book ends*."

"How exciting! It's like 'The Dream of the Rood.'" Jane resumed cleaning up after her daughter. Lee was abruptly oppressed by a belief that he had made her life harder to bear.

He said, "The girl must have been you because you're the only person I know who likes to have their back rubbed."

"You find my neck touching?"

"Well for God's sake, I can't be held accountable for the people I meet in dreams. I don't invite them." He was safe, of course, as long as they stayed away from the real issue, which was why he had told her the dream at all. "That girl means nothing to me now. In the dream obviously I was still in high school and hadn't met you. I remember sitting there and wondering, because it was such a long movie, if my mother would give me hell when I got back."

"I say, it's a very exciting dream. How far *are* you in Proust?"

"Sodom and Gomorrah." It occurred to him, what a queer mediocre thing it was, to scorn the English title yet not dare pronunciation of the French, and apropos of this self-revelation he said, "I'll never get out; I'm just the sort of person who begins Proust and can't finish. Lowest of the low. The humiliated and oppressed. Won't even tell his wife what his day was like." He changed his tone. "Which is better—to finish *Remembrance of Things Past*, or to never begin it?"

Unexpectedly, so profound was her fatigue, she did not recognize the question as a piece of sport rhetoric, and, after a moment's thought, seriously answered, "To finish it."

Then she turned, and her lovely pale face—in photographs like a white water-smoothed stone, so little did the indentations and markings of it have harshness—lengthened, and the space between her eyebrows creased vertically; into the kitchen she shouted, "*Jane!* What are you *doing?*"

While they had been talking, the child had been keeping herself quiet with the sugar bowl. It was a new trick of hers, to push a chair and climb up on it; in this way a new world, a fresh stratum of things, was made available to her curiosity. The sugar bowl, plump Swedish pewter, lived casually on the counter of a waist-high cabinet, near the wall. Little Jane had taken and inverted it, and with an eerie, repetitious, patient dabbling motion had reduced the one shining Alp to a system of low ranges. She paid no attention to her mother's shout, but when her parents drew closer and sighed together, she quickly turned her face toward

: 147 :

them as if for admiration, her chin and lips frosted. Her upper lip, when she smiled, curved like the handlebar of a bicycle. The sight of her incredibly many, perfect, blue, inturned teeth struck joy into Lee's heart.

With an audience now, little Jane accelerated her work. Her right hand, unattended by her eyes, which remained with her parents, scrabbled in a panicky way among the white drifts and then, palm down, swept a quantity onto the floor, where it hit with a sound like one stroke of a drummer's brush. On the spatter-pattern linoleum the grains of sugar were scarcely visible. The child looked down, wondering where they had gone.

"Damn you," his wife said to Lee, "you never do a damn thing to help. Now, why can't you play with her a minute? You're her father. *I'm* not going to clean it up." She walked out of the kitchen.

"I *do* play with her," he said, helplessly amiable (he understood his wife so well, divined so exactly what confused pain the scattered sugar caused her heart, as neatness-loving as her mother's), although he recognized that in her distraught state his keeping cheerful figured as mockery of her, one more cross to carry toward the day's end.

Lee asked his daughter, "Want to run around?"

Jane hunched her shoulders and threw back her head, her sugar-gritty teeth gleefully clenched. "Pay roun," she said, wagging her hand on her wrist.

He made the circular motion she had intended, and said, "In a minute. Now we must help poor Mommy." With two sheets of typing paper, using one as a brush and the other as a pan, he cleaned up what she had spilled on the counter, reaching around her, since she kept her position standing on the chair. Her breath floated randomly, like a butterfly, on his forearms as he swept. They seemed two conspirators. He folded the pan into a chute and returned the sugar to the bowl. Then there was the sugar on the floor—when you moved your feet, atoms of it crackled. He stooped, the two pieces of paper in his hands, knowing they wouldn't quite do.

Jane whimpered and recklessly jogged her body up and down on her legs, making the chair tip and slap the cabinet. "*Jane*," he said.

"Pay roun," the girl whined feebly, her strength sapped by frustration.

"*What?*" his wife answered from the living room in a voice as cross as his. She had fought giving the baby her name, but he had insisted; there was no other woman's name he liked, he had said.

"Nothing, I was shouting at the kid. She was going to throw herself off the chair. She wants to play Round."

"Well, why don't you? She's had an awfully dismal day. I don't think we make her happy enough."

"O.K., dammit. I will." He crumpled the sheets of paper and stuffed them into the wastepaper can, letting the collected sugar fly where it would.

Round was a simple game. Jane ran from the sofa in one room to the bed in the other, through the high white double doorway, with pilasters, that had persuaded them to take the small apartment. He chased her. When his hands nicked her bottom or touched her swollen waist, she laughed wildly her double laugh, which originated deep in her lungs and ricocheted, shrill, off her palate. Lee's problem was to avoid overtaking her, in the great length of his strides, and stepping on her. When she wobbled or slowed, he clapped twice or thrice, to give her the sense of his hands right behind her ears, like two nipping birds. If she toppled, he swiftly picked her up, tickling her briefly if she seemed stunned or indignant. When she reached the bed—two low couches, box springs on short legs, set side by side and made up as one—he leapfrogged over her and fell full-length on the mattresses. This, for him, was the strenuous part of the game. Jane, finding herself between her father's ankles after the rush of his body above her head, laughed her loudest, pivoted, and ran the other way, flailing her arms, which she held so stiffly the elbows were indentations. At the sofa end of the track there could be no leapfrogging. Lee merely stopped and stood with his back toward her until the little girl calculated she dare make a break for it. Her irises swivelled in their blue whites; it was the first strategy of her life. The instant she decided to move, her bottled excitement burst forth; as she clumped precipitately toward the high white arch laughter threatened to upend her world. The game lasted until the child's bath. Big Jane, for the first time that day free of her daughter, was not hurrying toward this moment.

After four times back and forth Lee was exhausted and damp. He flopped on the bed the fifth time and instead of rising rolled onto his back. This was ruining the crease in his pants. His daughter, having started off, felt his absence behind her and halted. Her mother was coming from the kitchen, carrying washed diapers and a dust brush. Like her own mother, big Jane held a cigarette in the left corner of her mouth. Her left eye fluttered against the smoke. Lee's mother-in-law was shorter than his wife, paler, more sarcastic—very different, he had thought. But this habit was hers right down to the tilt of the cigarette and the droop of the neglected ash. Looking, Lee saw that as Jane squinted, the white skin at the outside corner of her eye crinkled finely, as dry as her mother's, and that his wife's lids were touched with the lashless, grainy, humiliated quality of the lids of the middle-aged woman he had met not a dozen times, mostly in Indianapolis, where she kept a huge brick house spotlessly clean and sipped sherry from breakfast to bed. All unknowing he had married her.

Jane, as she passed him, glanced down with an untypical, sardonic, cigarette-stitched expression. By shifting his head on the pillow he could watch her in the bathroom. She turned her back to hang the diapers on a brown cord strung between mirror and window. This was more his Jane: the wide rounded shoulders, the back like two halves of a peach, the big thighs, the narrow ankles. In the mirror her face, straining up as she attached the clothespins, showed age and pallor. It was as if there could exist a coin one side of which wears thin while the other keeps all the gloss and contour of the minting.

"Da-*tee*." A coral flush had overspread his daughter's face; in another moment she would whimper and throw herself on the floor.

With an ostentatious groan—he didn't know which

of his women he was rebuking—Lee rose from the bed and chased his daughter again. Then they played in the living room with the bolsters, two prism-shaped pieces of foam rubber that served as a back to the sofa, an uncomfortable modernist slab that could, when a relative visited, be used for sleeping. Stood on end, the stiff bolsters were about the baby's height, and little Jane hugged them like brothers, and preferred them to dolls. Though to her human-sized, they were light enough to lift. Especially she loved to unzip the skin of mongrel linen fabric and prod with her finger the grayish, buoyant flesh beneath.

Catching them at this, big Jane said, "It kills me, it just is more depressing than anything she does, the way she's always trying to undress those bolsters. Don't en*cour*age her at it."

"I don't. It's not my idea. It was *you* who took the covers to the Launderette so she saw them naked. It made a big impression. It's a state of primal innocence she wants to get them back to."

Wavering between quarrel and honest discussion— that there was a way of "talking things out" was an idea she had inherited from her father, a rigorously liberal civic leader and committeeman—she chose discussion. "It's not just those bolsters, you know. About three times a day she takes all the books out of their jackets. And spills matches in a little heap. You have no idea how much cleaning up I have to do to keep this place from looking like a pigpen. Yesterday I was in the bathroom washing my hair and when I came out she had gotten our camera open. I guess the whole roll's exposed. I put it back. Today she wanted to get the works out of the music box and threw a tantrum. And I don't know how often she brings those nasty frustrating little Chinese eggs you got her to me and says, 'Opo. Opo.' "

Reminded of the word, little Jane said, of a bolster, "Opo, opo." The zipper was stuck.

"Japanese," Lee said. "Those eggs were made in Genuine Occupied Japan. They're antiques." The child's being balked by the zipper preyed on his nerves. He hated fiddling with things like zippers caught on tiny strips of cloth. It was like squinting into a specific detail of Hell. Further, as he leaned back on the bolsterless sofa to rest his neck against the wall, he was irritated to feel the glass-capped legs skid on the uneven floor. "It's a very healthy instinct," he went on. "She's an empiricist. She's throwing open doors long locked by superstition."

Jane said, "I looked up 'unwrapping instinct' in Spock and the only thing in the index was 'underweight.' " Her tone was listless and humorous, and for the moment this concession put the family, to Lee's mind, as right as three Japanese eggs, each inside the other.

His wife gave his daughter her bath as day turned to evening. He had to go into the bathroom himself and while there studied the scene. The child's silky body, where immersed, was of a graver tint than that of her skin smarting in air. Two new cakes of unwrapped soap drifted around her. When her mother put a washrag to her face, blinding and scratching her, her fingers turned pale green with the pressure of her grip on the edge of the tub. She didn't cry, though. "She seems to like her bath better now," he said.

"She loves it. From five on, until you come, she talks about it. Daddy. Bath. Omelet."

"Omma net," his daughter said, biting her lower lip in a smile for him.

It had become, in one of those delicate mutations of routine whereby Jane shifted duties to him, his job to feed the little girl. The child's soft mouth had been burned and she was wary; the sample bites Lee took to show her that the food was safe robbed of sharpness his appetite for his own dinner. Foreknowledge of the emotion caused in his wife by the sight of half-clean plates and half-full cups led him to complete little Jane's portion of tomato juice, omelet-with-toast, and, for dessert, applesauce. Handling the tiny cup and tiny knife and fork and spoon set his stomach slightly on edge. Though not fussy about food, he was disturbed by eating implements of improper weight or length. Jane, hidden in the kitchen, was unable to see, or if she had seen, to appreciate—for all their three years of marriage, she had a stunted awareness of his niceties—the discomfort he was giving himself. This annoyed him.

So he was unfortunately brusque with little Jane's bottle. Ideally the bottle was the happiest part of the meal. Steaming and dewy, it soared, white angel, out of the trembling pan, via Mommy's hands, with a kiss, into hers. She grabbed it, and Lee, his hand behind her head, steered her toward the bedroom and her crib.

"Nice maugham," she said, conscientiously echoing the infinity of times they had told her that the bottle was nice and warm.

Having lifted her into the crib and seen her root the bottle in her mouth, he dropped the fuzzy pink blanket over her and left quickly, gently closing the doors and sealing her into the darkness that was to merge with sleep. It was no doubt this quickness that undid the process. Though the child was drugged with heated milk, she still noticed a slight.

He suspected this at the time. When, their own meal barely begun, the crib springs creaked unmistakably, he said, "Son of a bitch." Stan Lomax, on their faint radio, was giving an account of Williams' latest verbal outrage; Lee was desperate to hear every word. Like many Americans he was spiritually dependent on Ted Williams. He asked his wife, "God damn it, doesn't that kid do anything in the day? Didn't you take her to the park? Why isn't she worn out?"

The one answer to this could be his own getting up, after a silence, and going in to wait out the baby's insomnia. The hollow goodness of the act, like a coin given to a beggar with embarrassment, infuriated his tongue: "I work like a fool all day and come home and run the kid up and down until my legs ache and I have a headache and then I can't even eat my pork chop in peace."

In the aquarium of the dark room his child's face floated spectrally, and her eyes seemed discrete pools of the distant, shy power that had put them all there, and had made these walls, and the single tree outside, showing the first stages of leaf under the yellow night sky of New York. "Do you want to go on the big bed?"

"Big—*bed!*"

"O.K."

"Ogay."

Adjusting to the lack of light, he perceived that the bottle, nested in a crumpled sheet, was drained. Little Jane had been standing in her crib, one foot on the edge, as in ballet school. For two weeks she had been gathering nerve for the time she would climb the crib's wall and drop free outside. He lifted her out, breathing "Ooh, *heavy*," and took her to the wide low bed made of two beds. She clung to the fuzzy blanket —with milk, her main soporific.

Beside her on the bed, he began their story. "Once upon a time, in the big, big woods—" She flipped ecstatically at the known cadence. "Now you relax. There was a tiny little creature name of Barry Mouse."

"Mouff!" she cried, and sat straight up, as if she had heard one. She looked down at him for confirmation.

"Barry Mouse," he said. "And one day when Barry Mouse was walking through the woods, he came to a great big tree, and in the top of the great big tree what do you think there was?"

At last she yielded to the insistent pressure of his hand and fell back, her heavy blond head sinking into the pillow. He repeated, "What do you think there was?"

"Owl."

"That's right. Up at the top of the tree there was an owl, and the owl said, 'I'm going to eat you, Barry Mouse.' And Barry Mouse said, 'No, no.' So Owl said, 'O.K., then why don't you *hop* on my *back* and we'll *fly* to the *moon?*' And so Barry Mouse hopped on Owl's back and awaay they went—"

Jane turned on her side, so her great face was an inch from his. She giggled and drummed her feet against his abdomen, solidly. Neither Lee nor his wife, who shared the one bedtime story, had ever worked out what happened on the moon. Once the owl and the mouse were aloft, their imaginations collapsed. Knowing his voice daren't stop now, when her state was possibly transitional and he felt as if he were bringing to his lips an absolutely brimful glass of liquid, he continued with some nonsense about cinnamon trees and Chinese maidens, no longer bothering to keep within her vocabulary. She began touching his face with her open mouth, a sure sign she was sleepy. "Hey," he murmured when one boneless moist kiss landed directly on his lips.

"Jane is so sleepy," he said, "because Daddy is sleepy, and Mommy is sleepy, and Bear is ssleepy, and Doll is sssleepy. . . ."

She lay quiet, her face in shadow, her fine straight yellow hair fanned across the pillow. Neither he nor his wife was blond; they had brown hair, rat color. There was little blondness in either family: just Jane's Aunt Ruth, and Lee's sister Margaret, eight years older than he and married before he had left grade school. She had been the fetching one of the children and he the bright one. So he imagined, though his parents loved them all impeccably.

Presuming his daughter asleep, he lifted himself on one elbow. She kicked his belly, rolled onto her back, and said in a voice loud with drowsiness, "Baaiy Mouff."

Stroking her strange hair, he began again, "Once

upon a time, in the deep, deep woods, there lived a little creature," and this time succeeded.

As he lowered her into her crib, her eyes opened. He
said, "O.K.?"

She pronounced beautifully, "O.K."

"Gee, she's practically epileptic with energy," he
said, blinded by the brilliant light of the room where his
wife had remained.

"She's a good child," Jane affirmed, speaking out of
her thoughts while left alone rather than in answer to
his remark. "Your dessert is on the table." She had kept
hers intact on the sofa beside her, so they could eat
their raspberry whip together. She also had beside her
an orange-juice glass half full of sherry.

When the clock said 7:50, he said, "Why don't you
run off to the movie? You never have any fun."

"All right," she said. "Go ahead. Go."

"No, I don't mean that. I mean you should go." Still,
he smiled.

"You can go as a reward for putting her to sleep."

"Venus, I don't *want* to go," he said, without great
emphasis, since at that moment he was rustling through
the paper. He had difficulty finding the theatre section,
and decided. "No, if you're too tired, no one will. I
can't leave you. You need me too much."

"If you want to, go; don't torment me about it," she
said, drawing on her sherry and staring into the *New
Republic*. When she had the chance, she worked at
being liberal.

"Do you think," he asked, "when Jane is sixteen,

she'll go around in the back seat of Chevrolets and leave her poor old Daddy?"

"I hope so," Jane said.

"Will she have your bosom?"

"Not immediately."

He earnestly tried to visualize his daughter matured, and saw little but a charm bracelet on a slim, fair wrist. The forearms of teen-age girls tapered amazingly, toward little cages of bird bones. Charm bracelets were *démodé* already, he supposed.

Lee, committed to a long leisured evening at home, of the type that seemed precious on the nights when they had to go out and be entertained, was made nervous by its wide opportunities. He nibbled at the reading matter closest to hand—an article, "Is the Individual a Thing of the Past?," and last Sunday's comic section. At Alley Oop he checked himself and went into the kitchen. Thinking of the oatmeal cookies habitual in his parents' home, he opened the cupboard and found four kinds of sugar and seven of cereal, five infants' and two adults'. Jane was always buying some esoteric grind of sugar for a pastrymaking project, then discovering she couldn't use it. He smiled at this foible and carried his smile like an egg on a spoon into the living room, where his wife saw it but of course not the point of it, that it was in love of her. He leaned his forehead against the bookcase, by the anthology shelf, and considered all the poetry he had once read evaporating in him, a vast dying sea.

As he stood there, his father floated from behind and possessed him, occupying specifically the curved area of the jawbone. He understood perfectly why that tall stoical man was a Mason, Booster, deacon, and Scout troop leader.

Jane, concentrating all the pleasures her day had withheld into the hour remaining before she became too dopey to think, put Bach on the record-player. As she did so, her back and arms made angles signifying to him a whole era of affection and, more, awe.

When she returned to the sofa, he asked, "What makes you so pretty?" Then, having to answer it, he said, "Childbearing."

Preoccupied with some dim speckled thinker in her magazine, she fondled the remark briefly and set it aside, mistakenly judging it to be a piece of an obscure, ill-tempered substance. He poured a little sherry for himself and struck a pose by the mantel, trying to find with his legs and shoulders angles equivalent in effect to those she had made putting on the record. As she sat there, studious, he circumscribed her, every detail, with the tidal thought *Mine, mine.* She wasn't watching. She thought she knew what to expect from him, tonight at least.

He resolved, *Later,* and, in a mood of resolution, read straight through the Jones Very section of Matthiessen's anthology. The poet's stubborn sensibility aroused a readerly stubbornness; when Lee had finished, it was too late, the hour had slipped by. By the clock it was 10:30; for his wife, it was after one. Her lids were pink. This was the sort of day when you sow and not reap.

Two hissing, clattering elves working a minor fairytale transposition, together they lifted the crib con-

taining the sleeping girl and carried it into the living
room, and shut the doors. Instead of undressing, Jane
picked up odds and ends of his—spare shoes and the
socks he had worn yesterday and the tie he had worn
today. Next she went into the bathroom and emerged
wearing a cotton nightie. In bed beside him she read a
page of *Swann's Way* and fell asleep under the harsh
light. He turned it off and thought furiously, the family's second insomniac. The heat of Jane's body made
the bed stuffy. He hated these low beds; he lay miles
below the ceiling, deep in the pit. The radiator, hidden
in the window sill by his head, breathed lavishly. High
above, through a net of crosses, a few stars strove
where the yellow gave out. The child cried once, but,
thank God, in her sleep.

He recalled what he always forgot in the interval of
day, his insomnia game. Last night he had finished D
in a burst of glory: Yvonne Dionne, Zuleika Dobson.
He let the new letter be G. Senator Albert Gore.
Benny Goodman, Constance Garnett, *David* Garnett,
Edvard Grieg. Goethe was Wolfgang and Gorki was
Maxim. Farley Granger, Graham Greene (or Greta
Garbo, *or* George Gobel), Henry Green. I was always difficult. You kept thinking of Ilka Chase. He
wrestled and turned and cursed his wife, her heedless
rump way on his side. To choke the temptation to
thump her awake, he padded after a glass of water,
scowling into the mirror. As he returned his head to
the cooled pillow, it came to him, Christian name and
surname both at once: Ira Gershwin. Ira Gershwin:
he savored it before proceeding. John Galsworthy,
Kathryn Grayson . . . Lou Gehrig, poor devil . . .

He and Jane walked along a dirt road, in high, open-field country, like the farm owned by Mark, his mother's brother. He was glad that Jane was seeing the place, because while he was growing up it had given him a sense of wealth to have an uncle attached to a hundred such well-kept acres. His relationship with Jane seemed to be at that stage when it was important for each side of the betrothal to produce external signs of respectability. "But I am even richer," he abruptly announced. She appeared not to notice. They walked companionably but in silence, and seemed responsible for the person with them, a female their height. Lee gathered the impression, despite a veil against his eyes, that this extra girl was blond and sturdy and docile. His sense of her sullenness may have been nothing but his anxiety to win her approval, reflected; though her features were hard to make out, the emotion he bore her was precise: the coppery, gratified, somewhat adrift feeling he would get when physically near girls he admired in high school. The wind had darkened and grown purposeful.

Jane went back, though the countryside remained the same, and he was dousing, with a lawn hose attached to the side of the house, the body of this third person. Her head rested on the ground; he held her ankles and slowly, easily turned the light, stiff mass, to wet every area. It was important that water wash over every bit of skin. He was careful; the task, like rinsing an automobile, was more absorbing than pleasant or unpleasant.

A Gift from the City

LIKE MOST HAPPY PEOPLE, THEY CAME FROM WELL inland. Amid this city's mysteries, they had grown very close. When the phone on his desk rang, he knew it was she. "Jim? Say. Something awful has happened."

"What?" His voice had contracted and sounded smaller. He pictured his wife and small daughter attacked by teen-agers, derelicts, coal men, beneath the slender sparse trees of Tenth Street; oh if only love were not immaterial! If only there were such a thing as enchantment, and he could draw, with a stick, a circle of safety around them that would hold, though they were on Tenth near Fifth and he forty blocks north.

"I guess it shouldn't be awful but it's so upsetting. Martha and I were in the apartment, we had just come back from the park, and I was making tea for her tea party—"

"Nnn. And?"

"And the doorbell rang. And I didn't know who could be calling, but I pressed the buzzer and went to the stairs, and there was this young Negro. It seemed strange, but then he looked awfully frightened and really smaller than I am. So I stood at the banister and he stood on the middle of the stairs, and he told me this story about how he had brought his family up from North Carolina in somebody else's truck and they had found a landlord who was giving them a room but they had no furniture or food. I couldn't understand half of what he said." Her voice broke here.

"Poor Liz. It's all right, he didn't expect you to."

"He kept saying something about his wife, and I *couldn't* understand it."

"You're O.K. now, aren't you?"

"Yes I'm O.K., let me finish."

"You're crying."

"Well it was awfully strange."

"What did he *do?*"

"He didn't *do* anything. He was very nice. He just wanted to know if there were any odd jobs I could let him do. He'd been all up and down Tenth Street just ringing doorbells, and nobody was home."

"We don't have any odd jobs."

"That's what I said. But I gave him ten dollars and said I was sorry but this was all I had in the house. It's all I did have."

"Good. That was just the right thing."

"Was it all right?"

"Sure. You say the poor devil came up in a truck?"
James was relieved: the shadow of the coal man had

passed; the enchantment had worked. It had seemed for a moment, from her voice, that the young Negro was right there in the apartment, squeezing Martha on the sofa.

"The point is, though," Liz said, "now we don't have any money for the weekend, and Janice is coming tomorrow night so we can go to the movies, and then the Bridges on Sunday. You know how she eats. Did you go to the bank?"

"Dammit, no. I forgot."

"Well, *dar*ling."

"I keep thinking we have lots of money." It was true; they did. "Never mind, maybe they'll cash a check here."

"You think? He was really awfully pathetic, and I couldn't tell if he was a crook or not."

"Well, even if he was he must have needed the money; crooks need money too."

"You think they *will* cash a check?"

"Sure. They love me."

"The really awful thing I haven't told you. When I gave him the ten dollars he said he wanted to thank you—he seemed awfully interested in you—and I said, Well, fine, but on Saturdays we were in and out all day, so he said he'd come in the evening. He really wants to thank you."

"He does."

"I told him we were going to the movies and he said he'd come around before we went."

"Isn't he rather aggressive? Why didn't he let *you* thank me for him?"

"Darley, I didn't know *what* to say."

"Then it's not the Bridges we need the money for; it's him."

"No, I don't think so. You made me forget the crucial part: He said he has gotten a job that starts Monday, so it's just this weekend he needs furniture."

"Why doesn't he sleep on the floor?" James could imagine himself, in needful circumstances, doing that. In the Army he had done worse.

"He has this *fam*ily, Jim. Did you want me not to give him anything—to run inside and lock the door? It would have been easy to do, you know."

"No, no, you were a wonderful Christian. I'm proud of you. Anyway, if he comes before the movie he can't very well stay all night."

This pleasant logic seemed firm enough to conclude on, yet when she had hung up and her voice was gone, the affair seemed ominous again. It was as if, with the click of the receiver, she had sunk beneath an ocean. His own perch, twenty-two stories above Park Avenue, swayed slightly, with the roll of too many cigarettes. He ground his present one into a turquoise ashtray, and looked about him, but his beige office at Dudevant & Smith (Industrial and Package Design) offered an inappropriate kind of comfort. His youth's high hopes—he had thought he was going to be a painter—had been distilled into a few practical solids: a steel desk, a sponge chair, a drawing board the size of a dining table, infinitely adjustable lighting fixtures, abundant draftsman's equipment, and a bulletin board so fresh it gave off a scent of cork. Oversized white tacks fixed on the cork several flattering memos from

Dudevant, a snapshot, a studio portrait of Liz, and a four-color ad for the Raydo shaver, a shaver that James had designed, though an asterisk next the object dropped the eye to the right-hand corner, to Dudevant's name, in elegantly modest sans-serif. This was all right; it was in the bargain. James's anonymity had been honestly purchased. Indeed, it seemed they couldn't give him enough; there was always some bonus or adjustment or employee benefit or Christmas present appearing on his desk, in one of those long blue envelopes that spelled "money" to his mind as surely as green engravings.

His recent fortunes had been so good, James had for months felt that some harsh blow was due. Cautious, he gave Providence few opportunities to instruct him. Its last chance, except for trips in the car, had been childbirth, and Liz had managed that with a poised animal ease, one Thursday at dawn. As the months passed harmlessly, James's suspicion increased that the city itself, with its steep Babylonian surfaces, its black noon shadows, its godless millions, was poised to strike. He placated the circumambient menace the only way he knew—by giving to beggars. He distributed between one and two dollars a day to Salvation Army singers, degraded violinists, husky blind men standing in the center of the pavement with their beautiful German shepherds, men on crutches offering yellow pencils, mumbling drunks anxious to shake his hand and show him the gash beneath their hats, men noncommittally displaying their metal legs in subway tunnels. Ambulatory ones, given the pick of a large crowd, would approach him; to their vision, though he dressed and looked like anyone else, he must wear, with Byzantine distinctness, the aureole of the soft touch.

Saturday was tense. James awoke feeling the exact shape of his stomach, a disagreeable tuber. The night before, he had tried to draw from Liz more information about her young Negro. "How was he dressed?"

"Not badly."

"Not badly!"

"A kind of sport coat with a red wool shirt open at the neck, I think."

"Well why is he all dolled up if he has no money? He dresses better than I do."

"It didn't seem *ter*ribly strange. You know he *would* have *one* good outfit."

"And he brought his wife and *seven* children up here in the cab of a truck?"

"I said seven? I just have the feeling it's seven."

"Sure. Seven dwarfs, seven lively arts, seven levels of Purgatory . . ."

"It couldn't have been in the cab, though. It must have been in the truck part. He said they had no furniture or anything except what they wore."

"Just the rags on their backs. Son of a bitch."

"This is so unlike you, darling. You're always sending checks to Father Flanagan."

"He only asks me once a year and at least he doesn't come crawling up the stairs after my wife."

James was indignant. The whole tribe of charity seekers, to whom he had been so good, had betrayed him. On Saturday morning, down on Eighth Street buying a book, he deliberately veered away, off the curb and into the gutter, to avoid a bum hopefully eying his lapels. At lunch the food lacked taste. The interval between the plate and his face exasperated him; he ate too fast, greedily. In the afternoon, all the way to the park, he maintained a repellent frown. When Liz seemed to dawdle, he took over the pushing of the carriage himself. A young colored man in Levis descended the steps of a brick four-story and peered up and down the street uncertainly. James's heart tripped. "There he is."

"Where?"

"Right ahead, looking at you."

"Aren't you scary? That's not him. Mine was really short."

At the park his daughter played in the damp sand by herself. No one seemed to love her; the other children romped at selfish games. The slatted shadow of the fence lengthened as the sun drew closer to the tops of the N.Y.U. buildings. Beneath this orange dying ball a yelping white played tennis with a tall Negro on an asphalt court, beneath the variously papered wall of a torn-down building. Martha tottered from the sandbox to the seesaw to the swings, in her element and fearless. Strange, the fruit of his seed was a native New Yorker; she had been born in a hospital on Twenty-ninth Street. He rescued her at the entry to the swing section, lifted her into one, and pushed her from the front. Her face dwindled and loomed, dwindled and loomed; she laughed, but none of the other parents or children gave a sign of hearing her. The metal of the swing was icy; this was September. A chill, end-of-summer breeze weighed restlessly on the backs of his hands.

When they returned to the apartment, after four, safe, and the Negro was not there, and Liz set about making tea as on any other day, his fears were confounded, and he irrationally ceased expecting anything bad to happen. Of course they gave the baby her bath and ate their dinner in peace; by pure will he was keeping the hateful doorbell smothered. And when it did ring, it was only Janice their baby-sitter, coming up the stairs with her grandmotherly slowness.

He warned her, "There's a slight chance a young Negro will be coming here to find us," and told her, more or less, the story.

"Well don't worry, I won't let him in," Janice said in the tone of one passing on a particularly frightening piece of gossip. "I'll tell him you're not here and I don't know when you'll be back." She was a good-hearted, unfortunate girl, with dusty tangerine hair. Her mother in Rhode Island was being filtered through a series of hopeless operations. Most of her weekends were spent up there, helping her mother die. The salary Janice earned as a stenographer at NBC was consumed by train fares and long-distance phone calls; she never accepted her fee at the end of a night's sitting without saying, with a soft one-sided smile wherein ages of Irish wit were listlessly deposited, "I hate to take it, but I need the money."

"Well, no, don't be rude or anything. Tell him—and I don't think he'll come, but just in case—we'll be here Sunday."

"The Bridges, too," Liz pointed out.

"Yeah, well, I don't think he'll show. If he's as new here as you said he said he was, he probably can't find the place again."

"You know," Janice said to Liz, "you really can't be so softhearted. I admire you for it, and I feel as sorry for these people as you do, but in this town, believe me, you don't dare trust anybody, literally *any*body. A girl at work beside me knows a man who's as healthy as you or me, but he goes around on crutches and makes a hundred and twenty dollars a week. Why, that's more than any of us who work honestly make."

James smiled tightly, insulted twice; he made more than that a week, and he did not like to hear he was being defrauded by pitiable souls on the street who he could see were genuinely deformed or feeble-minded or alcoholic.

After a pause, Liz gently asked the girl, "How is your mother?"

Janice's face brightened and was not quite so overpowered by the orange hair. "Oh, on the phone last night she sounded real high and mighty. The P.-T.A. has given her some job with a drive for funds, something she could do with pencil and paper, without getting up. I've told you how active she had been. She was all for getting out of bed. She said she can feel, you know, that it's out of her body now. But when I talked to the doctor last Sunday, he said we mustn't hope too much. But he seemed very proud of the operation."

"Well, good luck," James said, jingling the change in his pocket.

Janice shook her finger. "You have a good time. He isn't going to get in if I'm here, *that* you can depend on," she assured them, misunderstanding, or perhaps understanding more than necessary.

The picture was excellent, but just at the point where John Wayne, after tracking the Comanches from the snowbound forests of Montana to the blazing dunes of Border Country, was becoming reconciled to the idea of his niece cohabiting with a brave, James vividly remembered the bum who had wobbled toward him on Eighth Street—the twisted eye, the coat too small to button, the pulpy mouth with pathetic effort trying to frame the first words. The image made him squirm in his seat and pull away from Liz's hand. They decided not to stay for the second feature. Liz said her eyes smarted from the Vistavision. They were reluctant to go home so early; Janice counted on them to last out the double feature. But the service at the luncheonette was swift; the sodas—weak things, scarcely frothy at all, just tan liquid in a paper cone—were quickly drained; and the main streets of the Village, thronged with gangsters and hermaphrodites, seemed to James a poor place to stoll with his wife. Liz caught the attention of every thug and teen-ager they passed. "Stop it," he said. "You'll get me knifed."

"Darling. There's no law against people's eyes."

"There should be. They think you're a whore out with her pimp. What makes you stare at everybody?"

"Faces are *interesting*. Why are you so uninterested in people?"

"Because every other day you call up the office and I have to come rescue you from some damn bugaboo you've enticed up the stairs. No wonder Dudevant is getting set to fire me."

"Let's go home if you want to rave."

"We can't. Janice needs the money, the blood-sucker."

"It's nearly ten. She charges a dollar an hour, after all."

As they advanced down Tenth from Fifth he saw a slight blob by their gate which simply squinting did not erase. He did not expect ever to see Liz's Negro, who had had his chance at dinner. Yet when it was clear that a man *was* standing there, wearing a hat, James hastened forward, glad at last to have the enemy life-size and under scrutiny. They seemed to know each other well; James called "Hi!" and grasped the quickly offered hand, the palm waxy and cool, like a synthetic fabric.

"I just wanted . . . *thank* . . . such a fine gentle-man," the Negro said, in a voice incredibly thin-spun, the thread of it always breaking.

"Have you been waiting long?" Liz asked.

"No, well . . . the lady upstairs, she said you'd be back. When the man in the taxi let me go from the sta-tion . . . came on back to thank such wonderful peo-ple."

"I'm awfully sorry," James told him. "I thought you knew we were going off to the movies." His own voice sounded huge—a magnificent instrument. He must not be too elaborately courteous; Liz was terribly alive to

: 173 :

him in regard to vanity or condescension. She was unfair; his natural, heartfelt impulse at this moment was toward elaborate courtesy.

"You were at the police station?" Liz asked. Their previous encounter seemed to have attuned her to the man's speech.

". . . how I do appreciate." He was still speaking to James, ignoring Liz completely. This assumption that he, as head of the family, superseded all its other elements, and that in finding him the Negro had struck the fountainhead of his good fortune, made James panicky. He had been raised to believe in democratic marriages. Further, the little Negro seemed to need specifically maternal attention. He trembled softly under his coat, and it was not that cold; the night was warmer than the late afternoon had been.

The Negro's clothes, in the dimness of outdoors, did not look as shabby as James would have liked. As for his being young, James could distinguish no marks of either youth or age.

"Well, come on inside," he said.

"Aaaah . . . ?"

"Please," Liz said.

They entered the little overheated vestibule, and immediately the buzzer rasped at the lock, signalling that Janice had been watching from the window. She ran to the banister and shouted down in a whisper, "Did he get in? Has he told you about the taxi-driver?"

James, leading the group, attained the top of the stairs. "How was Martha?" he asked, rather plainly putting first things first.

"An absolute angel. How was the movie?"

"Quite good, really. It really was."

"I was honestly afraid he'd kill him."

They shuffled each other into the room. "I gather you two have met, then," James said to Janice and the Negro. The girl bared her teeth in a kindly smile that made her look five years older, and the Negro, who had his hat already in his hands and was therefore unable to tip it, bent the brim slightly and swiftly averted his head, confronting a striped canvas Liz had done, titled *Swans and Shadows*.

At this juncture, with these two showing these sinister signs of rapport, Liz deserted him, easing into the bedroom. She was bothered by fears that Martha would stop breathing among the blankets. "Before the doorbell rang, even," Janice talked on, "I could hear the shouting on the street—Oh, it was something. He said terrible things. And then the bell rang, and I answered it, like you had said to, and *he* said—" She indicated the Negro, who was still standing, in a quiet plaid sport coat.

"Sit down," James told him.

"—and *he* said that the taxi-driver wanted money. *I* said, 'I don't have any. I don't have a red cent, honestly.' You know when I come over I never think to bring my purse." James recalled she could never make change. There was usually an amount she was left owing them, "toward next time."

"I *tol* him," the Negro said, "there were these fine people, in this house here. The lady in there, she tol me you'd be *here*."

James asked, "Where did you take a taxi *from*?"

The Negro sought refuge in contemplation of his

hat, pendent from one quivering hand. "Please, Mister
. . . the lady, she knows about it." He looked toward
the bedroom door.

Janice rescued him, speaking briskly: "He told me
the driver wanted two thirty, and I said, 'I don't have a
cent.' Then I came in here and hunted, you know, to
see if you left any around—sometimes there's some
tens under the silver bowl."

"Oh, yes," James said.

"Then I went to the window to signal—I'm scared
to death of going downstairs and locking myself out—
and down on the street there was this crowd, from
across the street at Alex's, and it looked like when he
went back to tell the driver, the driver grabbed him;
there was a lot of shouting, and some woman kept saying 'Cop.' "

Liz reëntered the room.

"He grab me here," the Negro humbly explained.
He touched with his little free hand the open collar of
his red wool shirt.

"So I guess then they went to the police station,"
Janice concluded lamely, disappointed to discover that
her information was incomplete.

Liz, assuming that the police-station part of the story
had been told when she was out of the room, took this
to be the end, and asked, "Who wants some coffee?"

"No thanks, Betty," Janice said. "It keeps me
awake."

"It keeps everybody awake," James said. "That's
what it's supposed to do."

"Oh, no, Ma'am," the Negro said. "I couldn't do
that." Uneasily shifting his face toward James, though

he kept his eyes on the lamp burning above Janice's head, he went on, "I tolem at the station how there were these people. I had your address, cause the lady wrote it down on a little slip."

"Uh-huh." James assumed there was more to come. Why wasn't he still at the police station? Who paid the driver? The pause stretched. James felt increasingly remote; it scarcely seemed his room, with so strange a guest in it. He tilted his chair back, and the Negro sharpened as if through the wrong end of a telescope. There was a resemblance between the Negro's head and the Raydo shaver. The inventive thing about that design—the stroke of mind, in Dudevant's phrase— had been forthrightly paring away the space saved by the manufacturer's improved, smaller motor. Instead of a symmetrical case, then, in form like a tapered sugar sack, a squat, asymmetrical shape was created, which fitted, pleasingly weighty, in the user's hand like a religious stone full of mana. Likewise, a part of the Negro's skull had been eliminated. His eyes were higher in his head than drawing masters teach, and had been set shallowly on the edges where the planes of the face turned sideways. With a smothered start James realized that Janice, and Liz leaning in the doorway of the kitchen, and the Negro too, were expecting him to speak—the man of the situation, the benefactor. "Well, now, what *is* your trouble?" he asked brutally.

The coffee water sang, and Liz, after wrinkling her expressive high forehead at him, turned to the stove.

The Negro feebly rubbed the slant of his skull. "Aaaah? . . . appreciate the kindness of you and the lady . . . generous to a poor soul like me nobody wanted to help."

James prompted. "You and your wife and—how many children?"

"Seven, Mister. The oldest boy ten."

"—*have* found a place to live. Where?"

"Yessir, the man say he give us this room, but he say he can't put no beds in it, but I found this other man willing to give us on loan, you know, until I go to my job. . . . But the wife and children, they don't have no bed to rest their heads. Nothing to eat. My children are tired."

James put a cigarette in the center of his mouth and said as it bobbled, "You say you *have* a job?"

"Oh yes Mister, I went to this place where they're building the new road to the tunnel, you know, and *he* tol *me* as soon as I get in one day's work, he can give me that money, toward my pay. He ast if I could do the work and I said, 'Yes, sir, any kind of work you give I can do.' He said the pay was two dollar seventy cents for every hour you work."

"Two seventy? For heaven's sake. Twenty dollars a day just laboring?"

"Yes, pushing the wheelbarrow . . . he said two seventy. I said, 'I can do any kind of work you give. I'm a hard worker.'"

To James he looked extremely frail, but the happy idea of there existing a broad-shouldered foreman willing to make him a working citizen washed all doubts away. He smiled and insisted, "So it's really just this weekend you need to get over."

"Thas right. Starting Monday I'll be making two

seventy every hour. The wife, she's as happy as anybody could be."

The wife seemed to have altered underfoot, but
James let it pass; the end was in sight. He braced himself to enter the realm of money. Here Janice, the fool,
who should have left the minute they came home, in-
terrupted with, "Have you tried any agencies, like the
Salvation Army?"

"Oh, yes, Miss. All. They don't care much for fellas
like me. They say they'll give us money to get *back*,
but as for us staying—they won't do a damn thing.
Boy, you come up here in a truck, you're on your own.
Nobody help me except these people."

The man he probably was with his friends and family was starting to show. James was sleepy. The hard
chair hurt; the Negro had the comfortable chair. He
resented the man's becoming at ease. But there was
no halting it; the women were at work now.

"Isn't that awful," Janice said. "You wonder why
they have these agencies."

"You say you need help, your wife ain't got a place
to put her head, they give you money to go *back*."

Liz entered with two cups of coffee. Hers, James noticed, was just half full; he was to bear the larger burden of insomnia. The cup was too hot to hold. He set it
on the rug, feeling soft-skinned and effeminate in the
eyes of this hard worker worth twenty dollars a day.

"Why did you decide to leave North Carolina?" Liz
asked.

"Missis, a man like me, there's no chance there for
him. I worked in the cotton and they give me thirty-
five cents an hour."

"Thirty-five cents?" James said. "That's illegal, isn't it?"

The Negro smiled sardonically, his first facial expression of the evening. "Down there you don't tell them what's legal." To Liz he added, "The wife, Ma'am, she's the bravest woman. When I say, 'Let's go,' she said, 'Thas right, let's give oursels a chance.' So this man promise he'd take us up in the cab of the truck he had . . ."

"With all seven children?" James asked.

The Negro looked at him without the usual wavering. "We don't have anybody to leave them behind."

"And you have no friends or relatives here?" Liz asked.

"No, we don't have no friends, and until you were so kind to me it didn't look like we'd find any either."

Friends! In indignation James rose and, on his feet, had to go through the long-planned action of placing two ten-dollar bills on the table next to the Negro. The Negro ignored them, bowing his head. James made his speech. "Now, I don't know how much furniture costs —my wife gave me the impression that you were going to make the necessary payment with the ten. But here is twenty. It's all we can spare. This should carry you over until Monday, when you say you can get part of your salary for working on the Lincoln tunnel. I think it was very courageous of you to bring your family up here, and we want to wish you lots of luck. I'm sure you and your wife will make out." Flushing with shame, he resumed his post in the hard chair.

Janice bit her lip to cure a smile and looked toward Liz, who said nothing.

The Negro said, "Aeeh . . . Mister . . . can't find words to press, such fine *peop*le." And, while the three of them sat there, trapped and stunned, he tried to make himself cry. He pinched the bridge of his nose and shook his head and squeezed soft high animal sounds from his throat, but when he looked up, the grainy whites of his eyes were dry. Uncoördinated with this failure, his lips writhed in grief. He kept brushing his temple as if something were humming there. "Gee," he said. "The wife . . . she tol me, you got to go back and thank that man. . . ."

The Negro's sense of exit seemed as defective as his other theatrical skills. He just sat there, shaking his head and touching his nose. The bills on the table remained ignored—taboo, perhaps, until a sufficiently exhausting ritual of gratitude was performed. James, to whom rudeness came hard, teetered in his chair, avoiding all eyes; at the root of the Negro's demonstration there was either the plight he described or a plight that had made him lie. In either case, the man must be borne. Yet James found him all but unbearable; the thought of his life as he described it, swinging, blithe moron, from one tenuous vine of charity to the next— the truck driver, the landlord, Liz, the furniture man, the foreman, now James—was sickening, giddying. James said courteously, "Maybe you'd better be getting back to her."

"Iiih," the Negro sighed, on an irrelevant high note, as if he produced the sound with a pitch pipe.

James dreaded that Liz would start offering blankets and food if the Negro delayed further—as he did, whimpering and passing the hatbrim through his hands like an endless rope. While Liz was in the kitchen filling a paper bag for him, the Negro found breath to tell James that he wanted to bring his wife and all his family to see him and his missis, tomorrow, so they could all express gratitude. "Maybe there's some work . . . washing the floors, anything, she's so happy, until we can pay back. Twenty, gee." His hand fled to his eyes.

"No, don't you worry about us. That thirty dollars" —the record must be kept straight—"you can think of as a gift from the city."

"Oh I wouldn't have it no other way. You let my wife do all your work tomorrow."

"You and she get settled. Forget us."

Liz appeared with an awkward paper bag. There were to be no blankets, he deduced; his wife's stance seemed edged with defiance.

Talkative as always when a guest was leaving, James asked, "Now, do you know how to get back? For heaven's sake don't take a taxi. Take a bus and then the subway. Where is your place?"

"Aaaah . . . right near where that Lexington Avenue is."

"Where on Lexington? What cross street?"

"Beg pardon, Mister? I'm sorry, I don't make sense I'm so thrilled."

"What cross street? How far *up* on Lexington?"

"The, ah, hundred twenty-nine."

As James, with an outlander's simple pride in "knowing" New York, gave detailed instructions about where to board the Fourteenth Street bus, where to find the subway kiosk after so many stops, and how to put the token in the turnstile, the words seemed to

bounce back, as if they were finding identical information already lodged in the Negro's brain. He concluded, "Just try to resist the temptation to jump in a
taxicab. That would have cost us two thirty if we'd
been home. Now here, I'll even give you bus fare and
a token." Dredging a handful of silver from his coat
pocket, he placed a nickel and a dime and a token in
the svelte little palm and, since the hand did not move,
put two more dimes in it, then thought, *Oh hell,* and
poured all the coins in—over a dollar's worth.

"Now I'm penniless," he told the colored man.

"Thank eh, you too Missis, so much, and you Miss."

They wished him luck. He shook hands all around,
hoisted the bag with difficulty into his arms, and
walked murmuring through the door James held open
for him.

"Four blocks up, to Fourteenth Street," James called
after him, adding in a normal voice, "I know damn well
he'll take a taxi."

"It's awfully good-hearted of you," Janice said, "but
about giving all that money, I - don't - know."

"Ah, well," said James, doing a small dance step,
"money is dross."

Liz said, "I *was* surprised, darley, that you gave him
two bills."

"You *were?* These are times of inflation. You can't
buy seven air-conditioned Beautyrest mattresses for
ten dollars. He's shown a great gift for spending; he
ran through your ten like a little jack rabbit. We never
did find out where it went to."

Janice, Irishly earnest, still grappled with the moral
issue. She spoke more to Liz than to him. "I don't

doubt he needs the money—Oh, you should have heard the things that cabby said, or maybe you shouldn't. But then who doesn't need money? You and I need money, too."

"Which reminds me," James said. He looked at the electric clock in the kitchen: 11:20. "We came home, didn't we, around ten? Seven-thirty to ten—two and a half. Two and a half dollars. You can't change a ten, can you?"

The girl's face fell. "Honestly, I never remember to bring my purse. But you could owe me to next time. . . ."

"I hate to do that. You need the money." He couldn't believe the girl would take a surplus of $7.50 from him.

"That - I - do," Janice admitted cheerfully, gathering up her coat and a limp black book stamped simply with a cross. *Her mother*, James thought, and felt the prayers rising about them.

"Wait," Liz said. "I think in my purse. I lied to him when I said I had nothing in the house but the ten." They found the purse and were indeed able to piece together, out of paper and silver, the fee.

Spited, Janice said, "For your sakes, I sure hope he doesn't bother you again. This little island has more different kinds of crooks on it than you or I could imagine existed. Some of them could out-act old Larry Olivier himself."

"I really don't see how he can do this laboring job," Liz said, with a tactful appearance of agreeing. "Why, just that little bag I gave him almost knocked him over." When Janice was gone, she asked, "Do you think she expected us to pay her for the hour and a half she stayed to watch the Negro?"

"Heaven knows. I feel vile."

"Where?"

"Everywhere. I feel like a vile person."

"Why? You were fine. You were awfully, awfully good."

From her hasty kiss on his cheek he gathered that, surprisingly, she meant it.

Sunday, husk among days, was full of fear. Even in gay times James felt on this day like a nameless statue on an empty plaza. Now he dared not go out, either to church or to the newsstand. Last night's episode had the color of a public disgrace. The Negro was everywhere. James holed up in his inadequate cave. The walls seemed transparent, the floors sounding boards. The Negro's threat to return had smashed the windows and broken the burglar locks. Never on a morning had he wished so intensely to be back in Ontauk, Minnesota, his birthplace. The town had over seven thousand residents now, and a city manager instead of a mayor, and since the war the creek that ran through its center and drained its few mills had been robbed of its Indian name and called the Douglas MacArthur River; but the cars still parked higgledy-piggledy on the crooked, shaded streets, and he would still have a place, his father's son.

Liz and James lived four doors down from an Episcopal church. There was not an inch of air between the masonry of any of the buildings. When the church bells rang, their apartment quivered sonorously. Enveloped in this huge dead hum, he fought the picture of seven fuzz-haired children squeezed into the cab of a truck, roadside lights flickering in their faces, the dark of the Carolina fields slipping away, great whoring cities bristling and then falling back, too, and then the children dozing, except for the oldest, a boy of ten, who remained awake to stare unblinking at the bent-necked blue lights of the Jersey Turnpike, the jet carpet carrying them to the sorcerer's palace, where Harlem was choked with Cadillacs and white men on subways yielded their seats to colored ladies. James hated the Negro chiefly because he was tactless. Janice's mother, the sores of street beggars—this was misery, too, but misery that knew its limits, that kept an orbit and observed manners. But in his perfect ignorance the Negro was like one of those babies born with its heart in front of its ribs. He gave no protection. You touched him and you killed him. Now that he had found this Northern man—the promised man—so free with money, he would be back today, and again tomorrow, with an even greater gift of mumbled debts. Why not? Thirty was nothing to James. He could give away a flat three thousand, and then thirty every week—more than thirty, fifty—and he and Liz would still be richer than the Negro. Between him and the Negro the ground was unimpeded, and only a sin could be placed there as barrier.

By afternoon the focus of James's discomfort had shifted from the possibility that the Negro had told the truth to the possibility that he had not. Reliving his behavior in this light was agonizing. He shuddered above the depths of fatuity the Negro must have seen in his clumsy kindness. If the story had been a fraud, the impatience of James's charity was its one saving grace. The bits of abruptness, the gibes about the taxi shone in memory like jewels among refuse. The more he thought, the more he raged, aloud and privately. And the angrier he grew at the Negro, the less he wanted to see him, the more he dreaded him, an opponent invincibly armed with the weapon of having seen him as a fool. And those seven clambering children, and the wife bullying Liz.

He only wanted to hide his head in the haven of the Bridges' scheduled visit. They saw him as others saw him and knew his value. He would bask in their lucid external view.

Then mercifully it *was* dark, and his friends had come.

Rudy Bridges was also from Ontauk, Minnesota. He had been two classes ahead of James in the high school, a scholastic wonder, the more so because his father was a no-account who died of tuberculosis the year Rudy graduated. In the nine years since, Rudy's buttercup hair had thinned severely, but the spherical head and the chubby lips of the prig had remained constant. *His* great hopes had been boiled down to instructing three sections of Barnard girls in American history. His wife came from Maryland. Augustina was a pale and handsome woman with an uncompromising, uptilted nose that displayed its nostrils. She wore her abundant chestnut hair strictly parted in the middle—a madonna for the Piston Age. They had no children, and with elaborate managing, just enough money. James loved them as guests. In their own home, Rudy talked too much about his special field, domestic fiscal policy between Grant and Wilson, a desert of dullness where the lowliest scholar could be king. And Augustina, careful of the budget, went hungry and thirsty and inhibited everyone. Away from home she drank and ate beautifully.

James tiptoed into the bedroom with their heavy coats. Martha was cased in her crib like a piece of apparatus manufacturing sleep. He heard Liz talking and, returning, asked, "Is she telling you about how we're running the Underground Railway?"

"Why, no, James," Augustina said slowly.

"I was telling them the accident Martha had in the park," Liz said.

"Yeah, the poor kid just ran right into the swings," he said, no doubt duplicating the story.

"Now, James," Rudy said, "what is this mad tale about the Underground Rail*road?*" Years of teaching had perfected his speech habit of pronouncing everything, clichés and all, with artificial distinctness. Throughout James's recital of the Negro story he kept saying "Ah yes," and when it was over and, like Janice the night before, James seemed to have reached an insufficient conclusion, Rudy felt compelled to clarify: "So the chances are these seven children are going to show up in the middle of supper."

"Oh dear," Augustina said with mock alarm. "Do you have enough food?"

Rudy, beside her on the sofa, attacked the tale pedantically. "Now. You say he was well dressed?"

"Sort of. But after all it was Saturday night." James didn't get the smile he expected.

"Did you look at his shoes?"

"Not much."

"Would you say his accent was Southern or neutral?"

"Well, your wife's the only Southerner I know. His speech was so peculiar and high, I couldn't tell. Certainly he didn't talk like you. Or me."

"And at one point he used the word 'thrilled.' "

"Yeah, that got me, too. But look: there were odd things, but when a man is in such a dither anyway—"

Augustina broke in, addressing Liz. "Did James *really* just hand him thirty dollars?"

"Thirty-one and a token," James corrected.

Rudy laughed excessively—he had no sense of humor, so when he laughed it was too hard—and lifted his golden glass in toast. Augustina, to back him up, gripped hers, which was already empty. "James," Rudy said, "you're the soul of charity."

It was flattering, of course, but it wasn't the way he thought they should take it. The point really wasn't the thirty dollars at all; hard as it was to explain without seeming to ridicule Rudy's salary, thirty dollars was nothing.

"It doesn't seem to *me*, he said, "that he would have such an unlikely story, with so many authentic overtones, unless it were true. He didn't look at all like a Harlem Negro—his head was uncanny—and he seemed to know about North Carolina and the relief agencies—"

"Nonsense, James. There are a hundred—a thousand —ways of obtaining such information. For instance: he quoted thirty-five cents an hour as his old wage. Well, *you* could research that. *Is* thirty-five cents an hour standard pay in the cotton belt? To be frank, it sounds low to me."

"That was the thing," Liz said, "that made me begin to wonder."

James turned on her, surprised and stung. "Damn it, the trouble with people like you who are passed from one happy breadwinner to the next without missing a damn meal is that you refuse to admit that outside your own bubble anybody can be suffering. Of *course* people starve. Of *course* children die. Of *course* a man will pay a quarter an hour if nobody makes him pay more. Jesus."

"However," Rudy went on, "mere dollar-and-cents quotations mean very little; the relative value, purchasewise, of, for instance, ten cents, 'a thin dime'—"

James's harangue had agitated Augustina; her nostrils darted this way and that, and when she heard her husband's voice drone, she turned those marvelous staring apertures directly on him. Not insensitive, he slowly climbed out of his brain, sensed the heat in the room, and, the worst thing possible, fell silent.

The silence went on. Liz was blushing. James held his tongue, by way of apology to her. Rudy's brittle gears shifted, his mouth flipped open, and he considerately said, "No, joke about it as we will, a problem in sheer currency can very seriously affect real people. To take an example, in the states of the Confederacy in the decade after the surrender of Appomattox—that

is, from the year eighteen sixty-five to the year eighteen seventy-*four* . . ."

On Monday James's office was waiting for him. The
white-headed tacks made his personal constellation on
the cork. The wastebasket had been emptied. A blue
envelope lay on the steel desk. Otherwise, not so much
as a pen nib had been disturbed; the drawing he had
been working on when Liz called still lay by the telephone, its random placement preserved like the handi-
work of a superbly precious being.

He did his work all day with great precision, answering letters, making order. His office encouraged the illusion that each passage of life was on a separate sheet,
and could be dropped into the wastebasket, and de-
stroyed by someone else in the night. One job he gave
his mind was to keep the phone from ringing. Whether
the Negro came or not, with his tattered children or
not, from ten to five let the problem belong to Liz. It
was of her making. There should be, in a man's life,
hours when he has never married, and his wife walks in
magic circles she herself draws. It was little enough to
ask; he had sold his life, his chances, for her sake. The
phone did not ring, except once: Dudevant, effusive.

As he made his way home, through indifferent
crowds, the conviction grew that she had wanted to
call and had been balked by the cold pressure he had
applied at the other end of the line. He would find her
clubbed, and his daughter cut in two. He wondered if
he would be able to give a good enough description of
the Negro to the police. He saw himself in the station
stammering, blushing, despised by the policemen; had

it been their wives, they would have been there, knotting their fists, baring their teeth. Through this daydream ran the cowardly hope that the killer would not still be there, lingering stupidly, so that James would have to struggle with him, and be himself injured.

Liz waited until he was in the apartment and his coat was off before she communicated her news. Her tone was apprehensive. "He came again, when Martha was having her nap. I went to the stairs—I was terribly busy cleaning up. He said the man who promised to sell him the furniture wouldn't give him the beds if he didn't give him ten dollars more, and I asked him why he wasn't at his job, and he said something about Wednesday, I don't know. I told him we had given him all we could, and I didn't have a dollar—which was true; you went off with all the money and we have nothing for supper. Anyway, he seemed to have expected it, and was really very nice. So I guess he was a crook."

"Thank God," he said, and they never saw the Negro again, and their happiness returned.

Intercession

THE DROUGHT THAT HAD FALLEN ON ALL CONNECTICUT that summer fostered illusions. In the burned landscape of orange grass, the little red flags were hard to see, and the watered putting greens seemed hallucinatory ponds. Workmen were straightening the road nearby; rose-colored dust from the construction drifted across the first fairway. A road builder tried to wave Paul on. Paul shifted into second by way of defiance and racily cut in front of a truck bearing a pointed hill of blue spalls and continued in this loud gear a distance up the road that was not being improved.

He parked the car well over on the shoulder and lifted the borrowed bag of clubs from the back seat by the strap, inexpertly, so that the weight of their heads nearly spilled the clubs into the wild wheat that grew in the margin of the right of way. He was new to the game of golf in all its aspects. His wife's uncle had initiated him less than two weeks ago. On most of the days since, Paul had dutifully spent some time batting hollow, perforated practice balls back and forth on his own lawn. Their stunted flight was, very quickly, unsatisfying. You could not improve beyond a point; half the shots went straight, humming a little, and the rest dribbled off obliquely. Only on a golf course, with real distances and solid balls, could his achievement be measured. Nevertheless his wife had looked amazed when after lunch he threw her uncle's clubs into the car and left her alone with the house and child. He wrote the plot of a syndicated adventure strip, so she was used to having him home all day.

Inside a white clapboard shed, one entire side of which was painted with the figures 85¢, an old fat dark woman sat brooding like a prophetess, and a bin of soft drinks gave off with peculiar pungency the odor of refrigeration. "You're alone," she told Paul, and sold him a score card and pencil. Above her head hung stroboscopic watercolors of Gene Sarazan and Dr. Cary Middlecoff. On another wall a gray cardboard chart, like a pyramid of tuning forks turned sideways, demonstrated the progress of a defunct tournament. In the light of her eyes Paul suddenly felt that the shape of his heart was clumsily visible, as if behind bathroom glass. Doing anything in public for the first time—carving a roast, taking communion, buying a tuxedo—made the front wall of his chest feel fragile and thin. He didn't dare ask her where the first tee was, left the shed uncertainly, and walked around it.

As he emerged from behind the far corner a man not five yards away checked his swing and stared. Apologetically humpbacked, Paul scuttled, with a bobble of clubs, across the man's line of drive and took a place obsequiously far behind him. The man was freckled and iron-haired, except for red eyebrows; these stood out from his forehead like car-door handles. The gray hair furring the back of his neck in tiny controlled tufts led without sharp transition into a fuzzy cap, tactfully checkered, Scots in accent, its visor too short to shade his eyes except at noon. With one gloved and one bare hand he gripped a beautifully pale No. 2 wood. Paul wondered what made sandy men so smug. Blonde women were the same; these Paul could pardon, but not this old fop. With a swing as lucid and calm as the perfect circle that Giotto in one brush stroke drew to win Pope Benedict's commission, the Scotsman sent the ball deep into the fairway, within easy chipping of the green. His face was vacant, his soul flying with the ball. Then, so gently he might have been hooding a falcon, he fitted the golden head of his club with a chamois purse, and replaced the club in a bag on wheels, and pulled this cart after himself.

Paul took some considered swings at the puff of a dandelion. A potent repose, he imagined, was building in him. As the distant Scotsman took his iron shot, Paul planted a white tee in the patch of clay. When he straightened up, a tall kid with bony brown arms was standing close by. Though he had not noticed the boy before, Paul promptly said, "I guess you're ahead of me."

"I believe so." The niceness of the boy's diction combined oddly with his basketball sneakers.

"O.K. Go ahead."

"Shall we go around together?"

Paul was flattered to think that the boy had mistaken him for near his own age. Paul was greedy about looking young; at twenty-six, he looked twenty-three and wanted to look eighteen. "Thanks a lot, but you'd better go ahead. I'm pretty lousy."

Paul expected the protests an adult would have made, but the boy simply believed him. "All right," he said, with a monkeyish nod. "Thank you." The front of his T shirt, bearing the faded name of Alsace High School, hung as limp as wash from his shoulders. He turned to business; his arms above the elbow seemed no wider than the bone. The kid effortlessly sliced the ball high over the road, the workmen, and the cloud of pink dust, into the yard of a stucco house. "They can keep it," he announced contemptuously to nobody and teed up again. This time, he both hooked and topped; the ball streamed through the green grass near a watering hose, began to bounce rapidly when it hit a scorched area, and leaped a narrow drainage ditch. Paul regretted that he had not accepted the invitation. The kid, huffing indignantly through his nose, fetched yet another ball from the pocket of his bag. His third try went straight and hard.

"Couldn't be better," Paul offered.

"Yes, it could." The kid smiled at him with an unaccountable condescension, considering the performance he had just put on. "But I will accept it."

"That's good of you."

"What?"

"Nothing."

Still, Paul was so annoyed that, when his turn finally came, he pressed. The ball followed the route of the kid's second try: through the grass to his left, over the ditch, into the second fairway, which lay parallel to the first, going the other way. The elegant Scotsman was poised on the second tee. As Paul crossed over he could see the tiny figure against the trees check his swing.

Curiously, being alone did not make for calmness. Rather, the lack of any witness but the sun's steady eye induced panic. Paul hurried, though there was no one behind him. He left lost balls lying in the underwood and impatiently picked up disgraceful putts. He felt guilty, guilty about the most innocent things—about leaving his wife alone in the house for a few hours, about not working all day long like other men, about having grown up at all and married and left his parents alone together in Ohio, about being all by himself in this great kingdom of withered turf. The very volumes of air insecurely fenced by the multiple shifting horizons of the rolling course seemed freighted with guilt, pressing his ball down, making it fly crazy. His progress across the course became a jumbled rout. The fourth hole asked that you clear a tangled dry marsh, and the fifth, attacked from a tee that was a rubber mat beneath a plum tree, was out of sight over a crest, where the grass, never shaded, had turned a desolate salmon color and matted into the dirt. A weathered pink flag marked the place to aim at. Walking after his mediocre drive, he noticed, thirty yards to his right, a second pink flag, and when he descended into the shallow valley where the putting green had been laid, the flag in the hole said 7. He had skipped two holes. The approach to 5 had been to his right, and the approach to 6 must be intertwined somewhere, perhaps behind those spruces. The high-school kid, hitting a different ball at every third stride, was coming up *behind* him. "How're you doing?" he called.

"Awful," Paul answered.

"Stupid," the boy said to his ball as it skipped off the far edge of the green. He dropped another at his feet and swung more gingerly, with better success. He dropped a third and came within inches of the cup. "You *better* get wise," he told it.

Caught between the kid and the Scotsman, Paul had to keep going. The backs of his calves ached. His thumbs threatened to blister, and squinting into the sun had pinched his forehead. Paul didn't expect his body to turn querulous; not long ago it had accompanied him without complaint on any exertion, as forgiving and tireless as a dog at his heels. The Scotsman was setting out from the ninth tee, a little ziggurat by an elm. Paul slumped to the bench there. The slippery cuffs of his Dacron or whatever shirt kept unfurling. He glanced skyward to measure the day and noticed, on gauzy cirrus clouds near the sun, the explicable but eerie phenomenon of iridescence. The distant machines constructing the road made, all together, the noise of a bucket being cranked up a well.

The kid joined him. "What's your score?"

"I haven't kept it. I can't count that high."

"I never keep score on the first nine. My father told me, Don't bother. Just concentrate on getting tuned in. That's what I do." He whirled a club around and stared Byronically into an apple tree. "Do you know how

many holes of golf I play every day? How many do
you guess?"

'Six," Paul said.

"Forty-five or fifty-four. One day I played seventy-
two. How many do you play usually?"

"I don't know. I just started."

"Do you want to go around the next nine?"

The quaint precision of the boy's diction, which was
what Paul remembered most vividly of his earlier invitation, had relaxed somewhat. His chubby brown
face, cheerful and negroid below the eyes, was dis-
armed by his ears—cupped, fat-lobed, ambitious,
rather familiar. Studying the boy, Paul's eyes became
those of another kid and he recognized that his friend
was generally disliked. Braggarts always are at that
age. Paul had been stupid to see nothing unhappy in
a kid playing golf by himself all day like a retired
banker. His home, a glance at his new clubs confirmed,
was prosperous and fond, the type whose chaste, conceited, unpopular children poke around libraries and
luncheonettes and have hobbies intensely and never
quite hear the drum.

"Sure," Paul said, "but I warn you—I'm really poor."
He wondered about the boy's age. Height told nothing
any more. Paul guessed fifteen at the oldest; his elbows
were so broad, and he was so bluntly eager to go first,
so sure it was an advantage.

The kid stared down at the ninth green, which
seemed shorter than the two hundred yards advertised.
"I have to be careful," the kid said. "I usually overshoot
this one." But, though he tried twice, he did not. "Well,
not *too* rotten. See if you can get on."

Paul laughed; such frank competition tickled him. This age was so grainy, so coarse. How coarse he did not remember until he sliced his ball into an apple tree and was unable to find it among the fallen fruit. The kid found it for him and shouted, "Boy do you have great eyesight!" and, pinching his nostrils, cried for the world to hear, "Pee*yew!*"

Together they returned to the first tee. Paul had decided the secret was to make believe he was swinging at a hollow ball, casually, in his own yard. Though his drive was less good than the kid's, his approach was sweet, and he chipped on in three. By this time, the kid had several balls to play. Relieved at his fair showing, Paul felt friendly enough to confess, "Now if I could putt I'd have a par. But I can't putt."

"Let's see you."

"It's your honor. I'm closer."

"Go ahead. I want to see you put the ball right in. What's your grip?"

"It's nothing. Just a grip."

"O.K. now, just swing naturally. You're less than six feet away. A stinking baby could do it blindfolded."

Tense, Paul pushed too weakly, and the slant of the green dragged the ball off to the right.

"Look," the kid said, "be natural. You know how I putt? I'm just natural." He scrunched into an arabesque and, his hands braced against his belt, switched the club awkwardly. "And then just naturally put it in," he said, "bingo, like that. Look at me. I just step up to the ball"
—Paul's now. "I'm not *afraid*. I just look at the hole, take a natural grip, and . . . bingo."

As the kid led the way over a path through trees that were, with the heat and the insects, already starting to drop leaves, he said, "I got two fours on that hole. What did you get?"

"I suppose five. You sank my putt for me."

"We'll call it a five."

"If I'd done my own putt, I'd have had a four," Paul said.

"You want to hear some of my scores? Thirty-three on one round. Thirty-five another time. Seventy-two and seventy-three on one day, one in the morning and one in the afternoon. What's your best round?"

"I haven't played before, much. I never handled a club until two weeks ago."

"You know how long I've been playing? Guess."

"Seven years," Paul said.

"Eleven days."

"Really? You're very good, for eleven days."

"I like the game," the kid said. "I don't like it as much as fishing, but next to fishing I guess I like it best."

"You like fishing? Isn't it dull?"

"Dull, listen—there isn't a sport you can say that less of."

"Is it a sport? I think of a sport as taking skill and fishing just a lot of sitting," Paul said.

"Trout fishing? Are you kidding? Marlin fishing? Listen, there's nothing more skillful, believe me. Ted Williams is the most skillful baseball batter there is, and he's only a fair fisherman."

"I thought he was pretty good."

"Yeah. That's what the sportswriters say."

"Well, he probably isn't much good at shot-putting, either," Paul said.

"There's no comparison between those two things."

They crossed a little wooden bridge and came to the second tee. Paul asked, "Who goes first?"

"You can. Go ahead."

"Oh, no, you don't. It's your honor. You got two fours and I only got a feeble five."

"Go ahead. I want to study your swing."

To the right of the tee, for perhaps a city block, were woods. Meticulously Paul arranged his hands, squeezed, bent his left knee, inhaled, and kept his eye so intently on the sphere of dimpled rubber the intervening air seemed to petrify. Like a bird escaping, his swing fluttered through his hands. The mathematics of the parts had felt perfect, yet, in sum, the drive sliced into the woods, ricocheting forever into the green depths.

"You know what you do? You use your wrists too much. Use your arms. Here—let me see your grip. Is *that* it? Ugh. Now what's your thumb doing all the way over *here*? You going to be a contortionist or something when you grow up? Look how I hold it— natural. Be natural. Who taught you to stick your thumb down there?"

"My wife's uncle said, to keep the face of the club from turning." The fact was out: he had a wife. A little freeze of surprise did perhaps catch at the kid's features for a second, but immediately he recovered and went on the attack again.

"Who's he? A golf pro?"

"No, he just plays a lot."

"Boy, all these people with their crackpot systems. You listen to all of them, you'll go nuts. My *father*, and a guy he plays with who's pretty near a pro, he's as good as a pro, he was second in a tournament three years ago that was nearly statewide—*they* say just take a natural grip and pay no attention to everybody's weird systems." He teed up and said, "Swing nice and easy, with your arms pretty stiff. Like this." But the double load of talking and showing was too much for him, and his ball was badly topped. He turned and said to Paul, "That's your way. This is *my* way." His second drive was beautiful and long. "Now. Which way is better, your way or my way?"

"Your way."

"O.K." With a touching clownish grin, the kid bowed from the waist. "Never argue with Professor Shaw."

"All right," Paul said. "Which is better: Your way" —he pointed into the woods, where he had driven his first ball—"or *my* way." Paul had primitive faith; he really believed that, having thus committed himself, he would be rescued. During the moment after impact it seemed true, for the connection had felt solid, but while they watched, the ball, high as an airplane and piloted from within, curved more and more to the left and finally fell on the bank of ragweed and thistle near the road. The workmen had gone, their day done.

Professor Shaw said "That's *good?*" and walked off down the center of the fairway, retrieving his topped ball on the way, without looking back. Perhaps Paul's having a wife had scared him after all.

Paul had expected him to ask, "What do you do?"

"I think up the plot for a comic strip called Brace Larsen."

The boy's face would be blank.

"One of the Hartford papers carries it."

"You just think up the story and let somebody else draw it?"

Imagining this conversation while walking along with the dry grass in his eyes and the strap of the golf bag irritating his shoulder, Paul was losing patience. "That's right. I wanted to draw when I was a kid but the syndicate bought my ideas for other people to do up. They say anybody can execute; it's ideas that are rare."

Yet the boy's face would retain, clear as day, Paul's own conviction as a child that ideas were nothing and the actual drawing all that counted.

He was gone from the third tee when Paul reached it. It was a very short hole, 115 yards, backed by maples and flanked by fruit trees; the kid was walking toward the green, well to one side. Paul shouted, "Whajja get, Professor?" There was no answer. The strangeness of the illusion that the warps of the course had confronted him with himself of ten years ago had obscured the plain fact that he did not really like the kid, fat-lipped, daddy-loving brat. To be patronized and then evaded by a minor offended Paul's dignity as taxpayer, as husband, as father of a daughter to whom he was half the world, and as the creator of a plot which appeared in seventy-eight newspapers including one in Hawaii. It struck him as especially unjust, this daily extension of himself halfway across the Pacific yoked to this snub from the boy. Too annoyed to arrange his feet, Paul swung a mashie powerfully and with a start of pride and alarm that expanded his throat saw the ball coming down right on top of the kid. "Jesus look out!" he called. The kid turned and threw up an arm as if shielding his eyes from the sun, and remained in that pose some seconds. Either Paul's eyes lied or the ball passed right through his body. Heaven protecting fools.

When he got there, Shaw was among the maples, looking; dappled by shade, the planes of his face had the innocent frowning bluntness of an animal's.

Paul said "Gee, I'm sorry. I damn near killed you."

"You didn't even come close. Boy, are you wild." Paul liked the idea of his being wild. It was a long-lost kind of companionship, poking around together in dead leaves and the roots of brush. "I got a three on the last two holes," Shaw announced pleasantly. "This might be one of my better rounds."

"That's *won*derful. Hey, you needn't bother to hunt. The thing only cost fifty cents."

"What was the name on it?"

"I don't know."

"Was it Wilson?"

"I don't know. I doubt it."

"I just found a Wilson. I guess it's mine if it's not yours. Was yours new?"

"Not terribly."

"This makes three I've found today. A lot of these rich guys, they don't even *bother*."

They searched a bit longer. Paul, certain that what the boy had pocketed was what he was looking for, purposely smashed at small green plants and split young saplings by bringing his club down on their one fork.

"I give up," he said. "Let's go on. This leaves me one God-damn ball."

Professor Shaw glanced at him, somewhat offended by the swearing. "I can sell you a couple," he offered seriously. Paul disdained to answer.

At the fourth tee, the kid flubbed one into the marsh and teed up a second time and got across.

"If at first you don't succeed," Paul said, "try, try again."

"Huh?" He had, of course, heard. The boy's face went slack with such distinct fright that Paul momentarily relented, and addressed the ball. All he wanted was that his drive be brilliant; it was very little to ask. If miracles, in this age of faint faith, could enter anywhere, it would be here, where the causal fabric was thinnest, in the quick collisions and abrupt deflections of a game. Paul drove high but crookedly over the treetops. It was dismaying for a creature of spirit to realize that the angle of a surface striking a sphere counted for more with God than the most ardent hope.

"Boy, you'll never find that," the kid said. This time he didn't help Paul hunt. The ball must have landed in a breadth of desiccated swamp on the other side of the trees. The mud of the swamp, in drying, had cracked in neat rectangles; the weeds were filmed with dust that ballooned upward at a blow. As Paul circled, his ankles gathered burrs. His face and palms burned with sun and friction. Panic added its own blush; it was late, he should be home, he had no business here, he must hurry or lose the kid. He floundered to the edge of the short grass, reaching for his wallet—he would buy a couple of balls from the kid—and saw a white speck yards away, high and clear on a brown slope. He was so sure he had played into the swamp that it was several seconds before the feeling of the ball's placement in space being miraculous wore off. He went up to it, and it was absolutely his own. This luck gave him afflatus. He had outplayed the boy here; he was, when you came right down to it, the better golfer, being the older man, a resident of real life.

"I found it!" he called to Professor Shaw, who was walking past, on his way to the fifth tee.

"Why'd you bring it out so far?"

"I didn't bring it out. This is where it was. It cleared everything."

"I got another three on that hole."

"Well, who the hell *could*n't get a three if they took as many chances as you do? Hell, all you do is take about nine shots and then count the only three that are any good. If you played according to any rules, a stinking baby could beat you. *I* could beat you."

For the first time, the boy laughed; his teeth gleamed like the rims of two cups, but his averted eyes showed he had taken the wound. "I was demonstrating to you," he said.

Now Paul laughed. "Look," he said. "I'll bet you a dollar a hole I can beat you. If you play according to the rules I'll put up a dollar of mine against a beat-up golf ball of yours on every hole. That's five dollars you can make." He pulled out his wallet.

The boy was standing far enough away so that they had to shout across the intervening space; his image shimmied as a wave of heat came off the ground. "Keep your money," he said.

"You're afraid," Paul told him. "Rotten a player as I am, you know I'll beat you."

"No," the boy said in a strained voice and began walking.

"I'll catch up!" Paul shouted. "Easy money, Professor!" He waved the wallet above his head, but the boy wouldn't look.

Paul chipped onto the green and hastily putted twice. On the fifth tee, beneath the plum tree, looking across toward the two pink flags, ivy red in the rays of the declining sun, Paul felt exalted and certain. The kid, well on his way, a burnished and melancholy set of sticks, passed in front of the far flag, and Paul aimed for the double image. The ball, socked flatly, floated for a great distance in a leftward sweep and never rose, it seemed, three feet off the ground. That he had hooked did not diminish his conviction that he was destined to give the kid a deserved trouncing. The ball bounced once in the open and, as if a glass arm from Heaven had reached down and grabbed it, vanished. His eyes marked the exact spot in the air where it had disappeared.

He walked there. The scarcely sloping land where his ball should have been was unmarked by a bush or tree or ditch; on this table of stricken grass any hint of white would have glared. Hardly aware he had made a decision, Paul shifted the bag of clubs on his shoulder and walked toward the road, where his grinning car waited. It was almost suppertime; the little girl would be in the tub. He had never seen the fifth green, and inadvertently pictured it as paradisiacal—broad-leaved trees, birds, the cry of water. Professor Shaw might wonder why his friend failed to appear over the rise, but kids accept things easily; they haven't lived long enough to be sure of what's usual. The abandoned road-building machines stood among piles of dirt like extinct beasts paleontologists had uncovered. In all the landscape no human being was visible, and a fatiguing curse seemed laid on everything.

The Alligators

Joan Edison came to their half of the fifth grade from Maryland in March. She had a thin face with something of a grownup's tired expression and long black eyelashes like a doll's. Everybody hated her. That month Miss Fritz was reading to them during homeroom about a girl, Emmy, who was badly spoiled and always telling her parents lies about her twin sister Annie; nobody could believe, it was too amazing, how exactly when they were despising Emmy most Joan should come into the school with her show-off clothes and her hair left hanging down the back of her fuzzy sweater instead of being cut or braided and her having the crust to actually argue with teachers. "Well I'm sorry," she told Miss Fritz, not even rising from her seat, "but I *don't* see what the point is of homework. In Baltimore we never had any, and the *little* kids there knew what's in these books."

Charlie, who in a way enjoyed homework, was ready to join in the angry moan of the others. Little hurt lines had leaped up between Miss Fritz's eyebrows and he felt sorry for her, remembering how when that September John Eberly had half on purpose spilled purple Sho-Card paint on the newly sandpapered floor she had hidden her face in her arms on the desk and cried. She was afraid of the school board. "You're not in Baltimore now, Joan," Miss Fritz said. "You are in Olinger, Pennsylvania."

The children, Charlie among them, laughed, and Joan, blushing a soft brown color and raising her voice excitedly against the current of hatred, got in deeper by trying to explain, "Like there, instead of just *reading* about plants in a book we'd one day all bring in a flower we'd *picked* and cut it open and look at it in a *microscope.*" Because of her saying this, shadows, of broad leaves and wild slashed foreign flowers, darkened and complicated the idea they had of her.

Miss Fritz puckered her orange lips into fine wrinkles, then smiled. "In the upper levels you will be allowed to do that in this school. All things come in time, Joan, to patient little girls." When Joan started to argue *this*, Miss Fritz lifted one finger and said with the extra weight adults always have, held back in reserve, "No. No more, young lady, or you'll be in *serious* trouble with me." It gave the class courage to see that Miss Fritz didn't like her either.

After that, Joan couldn't open her mouth in class without there being a great groan. Outdoors on the macadam playground, at recess or fire drill or waiting in the morning for the buzzer, hardly anybody talked to her except to say "Stuck-up" or "Emmy" or "Whore, whore, from Balti-more." Boys were always

yanking open the bow at the back of her fancy dresses
and flipping little spitballs into the curls of her hanging hair. Once John Eberly even cut a section of her
hair off with a yellow plastic scissors stolen from art
class. This was the one time Charlie saw Joan cry
actual tears. He was as bad as the others: worse, because what the others did because they felt like it, he
did out of a plan, to make himself more popular. In the
first and second grade he had been liked pretty well,
but somewhere since then he had been dropped. There
was a gang, boys and girls both, that met Saturdays—
you heard them talk about it on Mondays—in Stuart
Morrison's garage, and took hikes and played touch
football together, and in winter sledded on Hill Street,
and in spring bicycled all over Olinger and did together what else, he couldn't imagine. Charlie had
known the chief members since before kindergarten.
But after school there seemed nothing for him to do
but go home promptly and do his homework and fiddle
with his Central American stamps and go to horror
movies alone, and on weekends nothing but beat monotonously at marbles or Monopoly or chess Darryl
Johns or Marvin Auerbach, who he wouldn't have
bothered at all with if they hadn't lived right in the
neighborhood, they being at least a year younger and
not bright for their age, either. Charlie thought the
gang might notice him and take him in if he backed
up their policies without being asked.

In Science, which 5A had in Miss Brobst's room
across the hall, he sat one seat ahead of Joan and annoyed her all he could, in spite of a feeling that, both
being disliked, they had something to share. One fact

he discovered was, she wasn't that bright. Her marks on quizzes were always lower than his. He told her, "Cutting up all those flowers didn't do you much good. Or maybe in Baltimore they taught you everything so long ago you've forgotten it in your old age."

Charlie drew; on his tablet where she could easily see over his shoulder he once in a while drew a picture titled "Joan the Dope": the profile of a girl with a lean nose and sad mincemouth, the lashes of her lowered eye as black as the pencil could make them and the hair falling, in ridiculous hooks, row after row, down through the sea-blue cross-lines clear off the bottom edge of the tablet.

March turned into spring. One of the signals was, on the high school grounds, before the cinder track was weeded and when the softball field was still four inches of mud, Happy Lasker came with the elaborate airplane model he had wasted the winter making. It had the American star on the wingtips and a pilot painted inside the cockpit and a miniature motor that burned real gas. The buzzing, off and on all Saturday morning, collected smaller kids from Second Street down to Lynoak. Then it was always the same: Happy shoved the plane into the air, where it climbed and made a razzing noise a minute, then nose-dived and crashed and usually burned in the grass or mud. Happy's father was rich.

In the weeks since she had come, Joan's clothes had slowly grown simpler, to go with the other girls', and one day she came to school with most of her hair cut off, and the rest brushed flat around her head and brought into a little tail behind. The laughter at her was more than she had ever heard. "Ooh. Baldy-paldy!" some idiot girl had exclaimed when Joan came into the cloakroom, and the stupid words went sliding around class all morning. "Baldy-paldy from Baltimore. Why is old Baldy-paldy red in the face?" John Eberly kept making the motion of a scissors with his fingers and its juicy ticking sound with his tongue. Miss Fritz rapped her knuckles on the window sill until she was rubbing the ache with the other hand, and finally she sent two boys to Mr. Lengel's office, delighting Charlie an enormous secret amount.

His own reaction to the haircut had been quiet, to want to draw her, changed. He had kept the other drawings folded in his desk, and one of his instincts was toward complete sets of things, Bat Man comics and A's and Costa Rican stamps. Halfway across the room from him, Joan held very still, afraid, it seemed, to move even a hand, her face a shamed pink. The haircut had brought out her forehead and exposed her neck and made her chin pointier and her eyes larger. Charlie felt thankful once again for having been born a boy, and having no sharp shocks, like losing your curls or starting to bleed, to make growing painful. How much girls suffer had been one of the first thoughts he had ever had. His caricature of her was wonderful, the work of a genius. He showed it to Stuart Morrison behind him; it was too good for him to appreciate, his dull egg eyes just flickered over it. Charlie traced it onto another piece of tablet paper, making her head completely bald. This drawing Stuart grabbed and it was passed clear around the room.

. . .

That night he had the dream. He must have dreamed it while lying there asleep in the morning light, for it was fresh in his head when he woke. They had been in a jungle. Joan, dressed in a torn sarong, was swimming in a clear river among alligators. Somehow, as if from a tree, he was looking down, and there was a calmness in the way the slim girl and the green alligators moved, in and out, perfectly visible under the window-skin of the water. Joan's face sometimes showed the horror she was undergoing and sometimes looked numb. Her hair trailed behind and fanned when her face came toward the surface. He shouted silently with grief. Then he had rescued her; without a sense of having dipped his arms in water, he was carrying her in two arms, himself in a bathing suit, and his feet firmly fixed to the knobby back of an alligator which skimmed upstream, through the shadows of high trees and white flowers and hanging vines, like a surfboard in a movie short. They seemed to be heading toward a wooden bridge arching over the stream. He wondered how he would duck it, and the river and the jungle gave way to his bed and his room, but through the change persisted, like a pedalled note on a piano, the sweetness and pride he had felt in saving and carrying the girl.

He loved Joan Edison. The morning was rainy, and under the umbrella his mother made him take this new knowledge, repeated again and again to himself, gathered like a bell of smoke. Love had no taste, but sharpened his sense of smell so that his oilcloth coat, his rubber boots, the red-tipped bushes hanging over the low walls holding back lawns all along Grand Street, even the dirt and moss in the cracks of the pavement each gave off clear odors. He would have laughed, if a wooden weight had not been placed high in his chest, near where his throat joined. He could not imagine himself laughing soon. It seemed he had reached one of those situations his Sunday school teacher, poor Miss West with her little mustache, had been trying to prepare him for. He prayed, *Give me Joan*. With the wet weather a solemn flatness had fallen over everything; an orange bus turning at the Bend and four birds on a telephone wire seemed to have the same importance. Yet he felt firmer and lighter and felt things as edges he must whip around and channels he must rush down. If he carried her off, did rescue her from the others' cruelty, he would have defied the gang and made a new one, his own. Just Joan and he at first, then others escaping from meanness and dumbness, until his gang was stronger and Stuart Morrison's garage was empty every Saturday. Charlie would be a king, with his own touch football game. Everyone would come and plead with him for mercy.

His first step was to tell all those in the cloakroom he loved Joan Edison now. They cared less than he had expected, considering how she was hated. He had more or less expected to have to fight with his fists. Hardly anybody gathered to hear the dream he had pictured himself telling everybody. Anyway that morning it would go around the class that he said he loved her, and though this was what he wanted, to in a way open a space between him and Joan, it felt funny nevertheless, and he stuttered when Miss Fritz had him go to the blackboard to explain something.

At lunch, he deliberately hid in the variety store until he saw her walk by. The homely girl with her he knew turned off at the next street. He waited a minute and then came out and began running to overtake Joan in the block between the street where the other girl turned down and the street where he turned up. It had stopped raining, and his rolled-up umbrella felt like a commando's bayonet. Coming up behind her, he said, "Bang. Bang."

She turned, and under her gaze, knowing she knew he loved her, his face heated and he stared down. "Why, Charlie," her voice said with her Maryland slowness, "what are you doing on this side of the street?" Carl the town cop stood in front of the elementary school to get them on the side of Grand Street where they belonged. Now Charlie would have to cross the avenue again, by himself, at the dangerous five-spoked intersection.

"Nothing," he said, and used up the one sentence he had prepared ahead: "I like your hair the new way."

"Thank you," she said, and stopped. In Baltimore she must have had manner lessons. Her eyes looked at his, and his vision jumped back from the rims of her lower lids as if from a brink. Yet in the space she occupied there was a great fullness that lent him height, as if he were standing by a window giving on the first morning after a snow.

"But then I didn't mind it the old way either."

"Yes?"

A peculiar reply. Another peculiar thing was the tan beneath her skin; he had noticed before, though not so closely, how when she colored it came up a gentle dull brown more than red. Also she wore something perfumed.

He asked, "How do you like Olinger?"

"Oh, I think it's nice."

"Nice? I guess. I guess maybe. Nice Olinger. I wouldn't know because I've never been anywhere else."

She luckily took this as a joke and laughed. Rather than risk saying something unfunny, he began to balance the umbrella by its point on one finger and, when this went well, walked backwards, shifting the balanced umbrella, its hook black against the patchy blue sky, from one palm to the other, back and forth. At the corner where they parted he got carried away and in imitating a suave gent leaning on a cane bent the handle hopelessly. Her amazement was worth twice the price of his mother's probable crossness.

He planned to walk her again, and further, after school. All through lunch he kept calculating. His father and he would repaint his bike. At the next haircut he would have his hair parted on the other side to get away from his cowlick. He would change himself totally; everyone would wonder what had happened to him. He would learn to swim, and take her to the dam.

In the afternoon the momentum of the dream wore off somewhat. Now that he kept his eyes always on her, he noticed, with a qualm of his stomach, that in passing in the afternoon from Miss Brobst's to Miss Fritz's room, Joan was not alone, but chattered with others. In class, too, she whispered. So it was with more shame—such shame that he didn't believe he could ever face even his parents again—than surprise that from behind the dark pane of the variety store he saw her walk by in the company of the gang, she and Stuart Morrison throwing back their teeth and screaming and he imitating something and poor moronic John Eberly tagging behind like a thick tail. Charlie watched them walk out of sight behind a tall hedge; relief was as yet a tiny fraction of his reversed world. It came to him that what he had taken for cruelty had been love, that far from hating her everybody had loved her from the beginning, and that even the stupidest knew it weeks before he did. That she was the queen of the class and might as well not exist, for all the good he would get out of it.

The Happiest I've Been

Neil Hovey came for me wearing a good suit. He parked his father's blue Chrysler on the dirt ramp by our barn and got out and stood by the open car door in a double-breasted tan gabardine suit, his hands in his pockets and his hair combed with water, squinting up at a lightning rod an old hurricane had knocked crooked.

We were driving to Chicago, so I had dressed in worn-out slacks and an outgrown corduroy shirt. But Neil was the friend I had always been most relaxed with, so I wasn't very disturbed. My parents and I walked out from the house, across the low stretch of lawn that was mostly mud after the thaw that had come on Christmas Day, and my grandmother, though I had kissed her good-bye inside the house, came out onto the porch, stooped and rather angry-looking, her head haloed by wild old woman's white hair and the hand more severely afflicted by arthritis waggling at her

breast in a worried way. It was growing dark and my
grandfather had gone to bed. "Nev-er trust the man
who wears the red necktie and parts his hair in the
middle," had been his final advice to me.

We had expected Neil since middle afternoon. Nine-
teen almost twenty, I was a college sophomore home
on vacation; that fall I had met in a fine arts course a
girl I had fallen in love with, and she had invited me to
the New Year's party her parents always gave and to
stay at her house a few nights. She lived in Chicago and
so did Neil now, though he had gone to our high
school. His father did something—sell steel was my
impression, a huge man opening a briefcase and saying
"The I-beams are very good this year"—that required
him to be always on the move, so that at about thirteen
Neil had been boarded with Mrs. Hovey's parents, the
Lancasters. They had lived in Olinger since the town
was incorporated. Indeed, old Jesse Lancaster, whose
sick larynx whistled when he breathed to us boys his
shocking and uproarious thoughts on the girls that
walked past his porch all day long, had twice been
burgess. Meanwhile Neil's father got a stationary job,
but he let Neil stay to graduate; after the night he
graduated, Neil drove throughout the next day to join
his parents. From Chicago to this part of Pennsylvania
was seventeen hours. In the twenty months he had
been gone Neil had come east fairly often; he loved
driving and Olinger was the one thing he had that was
close to a childhood home. In Chicago he was working
in a garage and getting his teeth straightened by the
Army so they could draft him. Korea was on. He had
to go back, and I wanted to go, so it was a happy ar-

rangement. "You're all dressed up," I accused him immediately.

"I've been saying good-bye." The knot of his necktie was loose and the corners of his mouth were rubbed with pink. Years later my mother recalled how that evening his breath to her stank so strongly of beer she was frightened to let me go with him. "*Your* grandfather always thought *his* grandfather was a very dubious character," she said then.

My father and Neil put my suitcases into the trunk; they contained all the clothes I had brought, for the girl and I were going to go back to college on the train together, and I would not see my home again until spring.

"Well, good-bye, boys," my mother said. "I think you're both very brave." In regard to me she meant the girl as much as the roads.

"Don't you worry, Mrs. Nordholm," Neil told her quickly. "He'll be safer than in his bed. I bet he sleeps from here to Indiana." He looked at me with an irritating imitation of her own fond gaze. When they shook hands good-bye it was with an equality established on the base of my helplessness. His being so slick startled me, but then you can have a friend for years and never see how he operates with adults.

I embraced my mother and over her shoulder with the camera of my head tried to take a snapshot I could keep of the house, the woods behind it and the sunset behind them, the bench beneath the walnut tree where my grandfather cut apples into skinless bits and fed them to himself, and the ruts in the soft lawn the bakery truck had made that morning.

We started down the half-mile of dirt road to the highway that, one way, went through Olinger to the city of Alton and, the other way, led through farmland to the Turnpike. It was luxurious after the stress of farewell to two-finger a cigarette out of the pack in my shirt pocket. My family knew I smoked but I didn't do it in front of them; we were all too sensitive to bear the awkwardness. I lit mine and held the match for Hovey. It was a relaxed friendship. We were about the same height and had the same degree of athletic incompetence and the same curious lack of whatever force it was that aroused loyalty and compliance in beautiful girls. There was his bad teeth and my skin allergy; these were being remedied now, when they mattered less. But it seemed to me the most important thing—about both our friendship and our failures to become, for all the love we felt for women, actual lovers—was that he and I lived with grandparents. This improved both our backward and forward vistas; we knew about the bedside commodes and midnight coughing fits that awaited most men, and we had a sense of childhoods before 1900, when the farmer ruled the land and America faced west. We had gained a humane dimension that made us gentle and humorous among peers but diffident at dances and hesitant in cars. Girls hate boys' doubts: they amount to insults. Gentleness is for married women to appreciate. (This is my thinking then.) A girl who has received out of nowhere a gift worth all Africa's ivory and Asia's gold wants more than just humanity to bestow it on.

Coming onto the highway, Neil turned right toward Olinger instead of left toward the Turnpike. My reaction was to twist and assure myself through the rear window that, though a pink triangle of sandstone stared through the bare treetops, nobody at my house could possibly see.

When he was again in third gear, Neil asked, "Are you in a hurry?"

"No. Not especially."

"Schuman's having his New Year's party two days early so we can go. I thought we'd go for a couple hours and miss the Friday night stuff on the Pike." His mouth moved and closed carefully over the dull, silver, painful braces.

"Sure," I said. "I don't care." In everything that followed there was this sensation of my being picked up and carried.

It was four miles from the farm to Olinger; we entered by Buchanan Road, driving past the tall white brick house I had lived in until I was fifteen. My grandfather had bought it before I was born and his stocks became bad, which had happened in the same year. The new owners had strung colored bulbs all along the front door frame and the edges of the porch roof. Downtown the cardboard Santa Claus still nodded in the drug store window but the loudspeaker on the undertaker's lawn had stopped broadcasting carols. It was quite dark now, so the arches of red and green lights above Grand Avenue seemed miracles of lift; in daylight you saw the bulbs were just hung from a straight cable by cords of different lengths. Larry Schuman lived on the other side of town, the newer side. Lights ran all the way up the front edges of his house and across the rain gutter. The next-door neighbor had a plywood reindeer-and-sleigh floodlit on his front lawn and a snowman of papier-mâché leaning tipsily (his eyes were x's) against the corner of his house. No real snow had fallen yet that winter. The air this evening, though, hinted that harder weather was coming.

The Schumans' living room felt warm. In one corner a blue spruce drenched with tinsel reached to the ceiling; around its pot surged a drift of wrapping paper and ribbon and boxes, a few still containing presents, gloves and diaries and other small properties that hadn't yet been absorbed into the mainstream of affluence. The ornamental balls were big as baseballs and all either crimson or indigo; the tree was so well-dressed I felt self-conscious in the same room with it, without a coat or tie and wearing an old green shirt too short in the sleeves. Everyone else was dressed for a party. Then Mr. Schuman stamped in comfortingly, crushing us all into one underneath his welcome, Neil and I and the three other boys who had showed up so far. He was dressed to go out on the town, in a vanilla topcoat and silvery silk muffler, smoking a cigar with the band still on. You could see in Mr. Schuman where Larry got the red hair and white eyelashes and the self-confidence, but what in the son was smirking and pushy was in the father shrewd and masterful. What the one used to make you nervous the other used to put you at ease. While Mr. was jollying us, Zoe Loessner, Larry's probable fiancée and the only other girl at the party so far, was talking nicely to Mrs., nodding with her entire neck and fingering her Kresge pearls and blowing cigarette smoke through the corners of her mouth, to keep it away from the middle-aged woman's face. Each time Zoe spat out a plume, the shelf of honey hair overhanging her temple bobbed. Mrs. Schuman beamed serenely above her mink coat and rhinestone pocketbook. It was odd to see her dressed in the trappings of the prosperity that usually supported her good nature invisibly, like a firm mattress under a bright homely quilt. Everybody loved her. She was a prime product of the county, a Pennsylvania Dutch woman with sons, who loved feeding her sons and who imagined that the entire world, like her life, was going well. I never saw her not smile, except at her husband. At last she moved him into the outdoors. He turned at the threshold and did a trick with his knees and called in to us, "Be good and if you can't be good, be careful."

With them out of the way, the next item was getting liquor. It was a familiar business. Did anybody have a forged driver's license? If not, who would dare to forge theirs? Larry could provide India ink. Then again, Larry's older brother Dale might be home and would go if it didn't take too much time. However, on weekends he often went straight from work to his fiancée's apartment and stayed until Sunday. If worse came to worse, Larry knew an illegal place in Alton, but they really soaked you. The problem was solved strangely. More people were arriving all the time and one of them, Cookie Behn, who had been held back one year and hence was deposited in our grade, announced that last November he had become in honest fact twenty-one. I at least gave Cookie my share of the money feeling a little queasy, vice had become so handy.

The party was the party I had been going to all my life, beginning with Ann Mahlon's first Hallowe'en party, that I attended as a hot, lumbering, breathless, and blind Donald Duck. My mother had made the costume, and the eyes kept slipping, and were further apart than my eyes, so that even when the clouds of gauze parted, it was to reveal the frustrating depthless world seen with one eye. Ann, who because her mother loved her so much as a child had remained somewhat childish, and I and another boy and girl who were not involved in any romantic crisis went down into Schuman's basement to play circular ping-pong. Armed with paddles, we stood each at a side of the table and when the ball was stroked ran around it counter-clockwise, slapping the ball and screaming. To run better the girls took off their heels and ruined their stockings on the cement floor. Their faces and arms and shoulder sections became flushed, and when a girl lunged forward toward the net the stiff neckline of her semi-formal dress dropped away and the white arcs of her brassiere could be glimpsed cupping fat, and when she reached high her shaved armpit gleamed like a bit of chicken skin. An earring of Ann's flew off and the two connected rhinestones skidded to lie near the wall, among the Schumans' power mower and badminton poles and empty bronze motor-oil cans twice punctured by triangles. All these images were immediately lost in the whirl of our running; we were dizzy before we stopped. Ann leaned on me getting back into her shoes.

When we pushed it open the door leading down into

the cellar banged against the newel post of the carpeted stairs going to the second floor; a third of the way up these, a couple sat discussing. The girl, Jacky Iselin, cried without emotion—the tears and nothing else, like water flowing over wood. Some people were in the kitchen mixing drinks and making noise. In the living room others danced to records: 78s then, stiff discs stacked in a ponderous leaning cylinder on the spindle of the Schumans' console. Every three minutes with a click and a crash another dropped and the mood abruptly changed. One moment it would be "Stay As Sweet As You Are": Clarence Lang with the absolute expression of an idiot standing and rocking monotonously with June Kaufmann's boneless sad brown hand trapped in his and their faces, staring in the same direction, pasted together like the facets of an idol. The music stopped; when they parted, a big squarish dark patch stained the cheek of each. Then the next moment it would be Goodman's "Loch Lomond" or "Cherokee" and nobody but Margaret Lento wanted to jitterbug. Mad, she danced by herself, swinging her head recklessly and snapping her backside; a corner of her skirt flipped a Christmas ball onto the rug, where it collapsed into a hundred convex reflectors. Female shoes were scattered in innocent pairs about the room. Some were flats, resting under the sofa shyly toed in; others were high heels lying cockeyed, the spike of one thrust into its mate. Sitting alone and ignored in a great armchair, I experienced within a warm keen dishevelment, as if there were real tears in my eyes. Had things been less unchanged they would have seemed less tragic. But the girls who had stepped out of these shoes were with few exceptions the ones who had attended my life's party. The alterations were so small: a haircut, an engagement ring, a franker plumpness. While they wheeled above me I sometimes caught from their faces an unfamiliar glint, off of a hardness I did not remember, as if beneath their skins these girls were growing more dense. The brutality added to the features of the boys I knew seemed a more willed effect, more desired and so less grievous. Considering that there was a war, surprisingly many were present, 4-F or at college or simply waiting to be called. Shortly before midnight the door rattled and there, under the porchlight, looking forlorn and chilled in their brief athletic jackets, stood three members of the class ahead of ours who in the old days always tried to crash Schuman's parties. At Olinger High they had been sports stars, and they still stood with that well-coördinated looseness, a look of dangling from strings. The three of them had enrolled together at Melanchthon, a small Lutheran college on the edge of Alton, and in this season played on the Melanchthon basketball team. That is, two did; the third hadn't been good enough. Schuman, out of cowardice more than mercy, let them in, and they hid without hesitation in the basement, and didn't bother us, having brought their own bottle.

There was one novel awkwardness. Darryl Bechtel had married Emmy Johnson and the couple came. Darryl had worked in his father's greenhouse and was considered dull; it was Emmy that we knew. At first no one danced with her, and Darryl didn't know how, but then Schuman, perhaps as host, dared. Others followed, but Schuman had her in his arms most often, and at midnight, when we were pretending the new year began, he kissed her; a wave of kissing swept the room now, and everyone struggled to kiss Emmy. Even I did. There was something about her being married that made it extraordinary. Her cheeks in flame, she kept glancing around for rescue, but Darryl, embarrassed to see his wife dance, had gone into old man Schuman's den, where Neil sat brooding, sunk in mysterious sorrow.

When the kissing subsided and Darryl emerged, I went in to see Neil. He was holding his face in his hands and tapping his foot to a record playing on Mr. Schuman's private phonograph: Krupa's "Dark Eyes." The arrangement was droning and circular and Neil had kept the record going for hours. He loved saxophones; I guess all of us children of that Depression vintage did. I asked him, "Do you think the traffic on the Turnpike has died down by now?"

He took down the tall glass of the cabinet beside him and took a convincing swallow. His face from the side seemed lean and somewhat blue. "Maybe," he said, staring at the ice cubes submerged in the ochre liquid. "The girl in Chicago's expecting you?"

"Well, yeah, but we can call and let her know, once *we* know."

"You think she'll spoil?"

"How do you mean?"

"I mean, won't you be seeing her all the time after we get there? Aren't you going to marry her?"

"I have no idea. I might."

"Well then: you'll have the rest of Kingdom Come to see her." He looked directly at me, and it was plain in the blur of his eyes that he was sick-drunk. "The trouble with you guys that have all the luck," he said slowly, "is that you don't give a fuck about us that don't have any." Such melodramatic rudeness coming from Neil surprised me, as had his blarney with my mother hours before. In trying to evade his wounded stare, I discovered there was another person in the room: a girl sitting with her shoes on, reading *Holiday*. Though she held the magazine in front of her face I knew from her clothes and her unfamiliar legs that she was the girl friend Margaret Lento had brought. Margaret didn't come from Olinger but from Riverside, a section of Alton, not a suburb. She had met Larry Schuman at a summer job in a restaurant and for the rest of high school they had more or less gone together. Since then, though, it had dawned on Mr. and Mrs. Schuman that even in a democracy distinctions exist, probably welcome news to Larry. In the cruellest and most stretched-out way he could manage he had been breaking off with her throughout the year now nearly ended. I had been surprised to find her at this party. Obviously she had felt shaky about attending and had brought the friend as the only kind of protection she could afford. The other girl was acting just like a hired guard.

There being no answer to Neil, I went into the living room, where Margaret, insanely drunk, was throwing herself around as if wanting to break a bone. Somewhat in time to the music she would run a few steps, then snap her body like a whip, her chin striking her chest and her hands flying backward, fingers fanned, as her shoulders pitched forward. In her state her body was childishly plastic; unharmed, she would bounce back from this jolt and begin to clap and kick and hum. Schuman stayed away from her. Margaret was small, not more than 5'3", with the smallness ripeness comes to early. She had bleached a section of her black hair platinum, cropped her head all over, and trained the stubble into short hyacinthine curls like those on antique statues of boys. Her face seemed quite coarse from the front, so her profile was classical unexpectedly. She might have been Portia. When she was not putting on her savage pointless dance she was in the bathroom being sick. The pity and the vulgarity of her exhibition made everyone who was sober uncomfortable; our common guilt in witnessing this girl's rites brought us so close together in that room that it seemed never, not in all time, could we be parted. I myself was perfectly sober. I had the impression then that people only drank to stop being unhappy and I nearly always felt at least fairly happy.

Luckily, Margaret was in a sick phase around one o'clock, when the elder Schumans came home. They looked in at us briefly. It was a pleasant joke to see in their smiles that, however corrupt and unwinking we felt, to them we looked young and sleepy: Larry's friends. Things quieted after they went up the stairs. In half an hour people began coming out of the kitchen balancing cups of coffee. By two o'clock four girls stood in aprons at Mrs. Schuman's sink, and others were padding back and forth carrying glasses and ashtrays. Another blameless racket pierced the clatter in the kitchen. Out on the cold grass the three Melanchthon athletes had set up the badminton net and in the faint glow given off by the house were playing. The bird, ascending and descending through uneven bars of light, glimmered like a firefly. Now that the party was dying Neil's apathy seemed deliberately exasperating, even vindictive. For at least another hour he persisted in hearing "Dark Eyes" over and over again, holding his head and tapping his foot. The entire scene in the den had developed a fixity that was uncanny; the girl remained in the chair and read magazines, *Holiday* and *Esquire*, one after another. In the meantime, cars came and went and raced their motors out front; Schuman took Ann Mahlon off and didn't come back; and the athletes carried the neighbor's artificial snowman into the center of the street and disappeared. Somehow in the arrangments shuffled together at the end, Neil had contracted to drive Margaret and the other girl home. Margaret convalesced in the downstairs bathroom for most of that hour. I unlocked a little glass bookcase ornamenting a desk in the dark dining room and removed a volume of Thackcry's Works. It turned out to be Volume II of *Henry Esmond*. I began it, rather than break another book out of the set, which had been squeezed in there so long the bindings had sort of interpenetrated.

Henry was going off to war again when Neil appeared in the archway and said, "O.K., Norseman. Let's go to Chicago." "Norseman" was a variant of my name he used only when feeling special affection.

We turned off all the lamps and left the hall bulb burning against Larry's return. Margaret Lento seemed chastened. Neil gave her his arm and led her into the back seat of his father's car; I stood aside to let the

other girl get in with her, but Neil indicated that I
should. I supposed he realized this left only the mute
den-girl to go up front with him. She sat well over on
her side, was all I noticed. Neil backed into the street
and with unusual care steered past the snowman. Our
headlights made vivid the fact that the snowman's back
was a hollow right-angled gash; he had been built up
against the corner of a house.

From Olinger, Riverside was diagonally across
Alton. The city was sleeping as we drove through it.
Most of the stoplights were blinking green. Among
cities Alton had a bad reputation; its graft and gam-
bling and easy juries and bawdy houses were supposedly notorious throughout the Middle Atlantic
states. But to me it always presented an innocent face;
row after row of houses built of a local dusty-red brick
the shade of flowerpots, each house fortified with a
tiny, intimate, balustraded porch, and nothing but the
wealth of movie houses and beer signs along its main
street to suggest that its citizens loved pleasure more
than the run of mankind. Indeed, as we moved at
moderate speed down these hushed streets bordered
with parked cars, a limestone church bulking at every
corner and the hooded street lamps keeping watch
from above, Alton seemed less the ultimate center of
an urban region than itself a suburb of some vast myth-
ical metropolis, like Pandemonium or Paradise. I was
conscious of evergreen wreaths on door after door and
of fanlights of stained glass in which the house number
was embedded. I was also conscious that every block
was one block further from the Turnpike.

Riverside, fitted into the bends of the Schuylkill, was not so regularly laid out. Margaret's house was one of a short row, composition-shingled, which we approached from the rear, down a tiny cement alley speckled with drains. The porches were a few inches higher than the alley. Margaret asked us if we wanted to come in for a cup of coffee, since we were going to Chicago; Neil accepted by getting out of the car and slamming his door. The noise filled the alley, alarming me. I wondered at the easy social life that evidently existed among my friends at three-thirty in the morning. Margaret did, however, lead us in stealthily, and she turned on only the kitchen switch. The kitchen was divided from the living room by a large sofa, which faced into littered gloom where distant light from beyond the alley spilled over the window sill and across the spines of a radiator. In one corner the glass of a television set showed; the screen would seem absurdly small now, but then it seemed disproportionately elegant. The shabbiness everywhere would not have struck me so definitely if I hadn't just come from Schuman's place. Neil and the other girl sat on the sofa; Margaret held a match to a gas burner and, as the blue flame licked an old kettle, doled instant coffee into four flowered cups.

Some man who had once lived in this house had built by the kitchen's one window a breakfast nook, nothing more than a booth, a table between two high-backed benches. I sat in it and read all the words I could see: "Salt," "Pepper," "Have Some Lumps," "December," "Mohn's Milk Inc.—A Very Merry Christmas and Joyous New Year—Mohn's Milk is *Safe* Milk—

'Mommy, Make It Mohn's!,'" "Matches," "Hot-point," "PRESS," "Magee Stove FEDERAL & Furnace Corp.," "God Is In This House," "Ave Maria Gratia Plena," "SHREDDED WHEAT Benefits Exciting New Pattern KUNGSHOLM." After serving the two on the sofa, Margaret came to me with coffee and sat down opposite me in the booth. Fatigue had raised two blue welts beneath her eyes.

"Well," I asked her, "did you have a good time?"

She smiled and glanced down and made the small sound "Ch," vestigal of "Jesus." With absent-minded delicacy she stirred her coffee, lifting and replacing the spoon without a ripple.

"Rather odd at the end," I said, "not even the host there."

"He took Ann Mahlon home."

"I know." I was surprised that she knew, having been sick in the bathroom for that hour.

"You sound jealous," she added.

"Who does? I do? I don't."

"You like her, John, don't you?" Her using my first name and the quality of the question did not, although discounting parties we had just met, seem forward, considering the hour and that she had brought me coffee. There is very little further to go with a girl who has brought you coffee.

"Oh, I like everybody," I told her, "and the longer I've known them the more I like them, because the more they're me. The only people I like better are ones I've just met. Now Ann Mahlon I've known since kindergarten. Every day her mother used to bring her to the edge of the schoolyard for months after all the other mothers had stopped." I wanted to cut a figure in Margaret's eyes, but they were too dark. Stoically she had gotten on top of her weariness, but it was growing bigger under her.

"Did you like her then?"

"I felt sorry for her being embarrassed by her mother."

She asked me, "What was Larry like when he was little?"

"Oh, bright. Kind of mean."

"Was he mean?"

"I'd say so. Yes. In some grade or other he and I began to play chess together. I always won until secretly he took lessons from a man his parents knew and read strategy books."

Margaret laughed, genuinely pleased. "Then did he win?"

"Once. After that I really tried, and after *that* he decided chess was kid stuff. Besides, I was used up. He'd have these runs on people where you'd be down at his house every afternoon, then in a couple months he'd get a new pet and that'd be that."

"He's funny," she said. "He has a kind of cold mind. He decides on what he wants, then he does what he has to do, you know, and nothing anybody says can change him."

"He does tend to get what he wants," I admitted guardedly, realizing that to her this meant her. Poor bruised little girl, in her mind he was all the time cleaving with rare cunning through his parents' objections straight to her.

My coffee was nearly gone, so I glanced toward the

sofa in the other room. Neil and the girl had sunk out of sight behind its back. Before this it had honestly not occurred to me that they had a relationship, but now that I saw, it seemed plausible and, at this time of night, good news, though it meant we would not be going to Chicago yet.

So I talked to Margaret about Larry, and she responded, showing really quite an acute sense of him. To me, considering so seriously the personality of a childhood friend, as if overnight he had become a factor in the world, seemed absurd; I couldn't deeply believe that even in her world he mattered much. Larry Schuman, in little more than a year, had become nothing to me. The important thing, rather than the subject, was the conversation itself, the quick agreements, the slow nods, the weave of different memories; it was like one of those Panama baskets shaped underwater around a worthless stone.

She offered me more coffee. When she returned with it, she sat down, not opposite, but beside me, lifting me to such a pitch of gratitude and affection the only way I could think to express it was by *not* kissing her, as if a kiss were another piece of abuse women suffered. She said, "Cold. Cheap bastard turns the thermostat down to sixty," meaning her father. She drew my arm around her shoulders and folded my hand around her bare forearm, to warm it. The back of my thumb fitted against the curve of one breast. Her head went into the hollow where my arm and chest joined; she was terribly small, measured against your own body. Perhaps she weighed a hundred pounds. Her lids lowered and I kissed her two beautiful eyebrows and then the spaces of skin between the rough curls, some black and some bleached, that fringed her forehead. Other than this I tried to keep as still as a bed would be. It *had* grown cold. A shiver starting on the side away from her would twitch my shoulders when I tried to repress it; she would frown and unconsciously draw my arm tighter. No one had switched the kitchen light off. On Margaret's foreshortened upper lip there seemed to be two pencil marks; the length of wrist my badly fitting sleeve exposed looked pale and naked against the spiralling down of the smaller arm held beneath it.

Outside on the street the house faced there was no motion. Only once did a car go by: around five o'clock, with twin mufflers, the radio on and a boy yelling. Neil and the girl murmured together incessantly; some of what they said I could overhear.

"No. Which?" she asked.

"I don't care."

"Wouldn't you want a boy?"

"I'd be happy whatever I got."

"I know, but which would you *rather* have? Don't men want boys?"

"I don't care. You."

Somewhat later, Mohn's truck passed on the other side of the street. The milkman, well-bundled, sat behind headlights in a warm orange volume the size of a phone booth, steering one-handed and smoking a cigar that he set on the edge of the dashboard when, his wire carrier vibrant, he ran out of the truck with bottles. His passing led Neil to decide the time had come. Margaret woke up frightened of her father; we hissed our farewells and thanks to her quickly. Neil dropped the other girl off at her house a few blocks away; he knew where it was. Sometime during that night I must have seen this girl's face, but I have no memory of it. She is always behind a magazine or in the dark or with her back turned. Neil married her years later, I know, but after we arrived in Chicago I never saw him again either.

Red dawn light touched the clouds above the black slate roofs as, with a few other cars, we drove through Alton. The moon-sized clock of a beer billboard said ten after six. Olinger was deathly still. The air brightened as we moved along the highway; the glowing wall of my home hung above the woods as we rounded the long curve by the Mennonite dairy. With a .22 I could have had a pane of my parents' bedroom window, and they were dreaming I was in Indiana. My grandfather would be up, stamping around in the kitchen for my grandmother to make him breakfast, or outside, walking to see if any ice had formed on the brook. For an instant I genuinely feared he might hail me from the peak of the barn roof. Then trees interceded and we were safe in a landscape where no one cared.

At the entrance to the Turnpike Neil did a strange thing, stopped the car and had me take the wheel. He had never trusted me to drive his father's car before; he had believed my not knowing where the crankshaft and fuel pump were handicapped my competence to steer. But now he was quite complacent. He hunched under an old mackinaw and leaned his head against the metal of the window frame and soon was asleep. We crossed the Susquehanna on a long smooth bridge below Harrisburg, then began climbing toward the Alleghenies. In the mountains there was snow, a dry dusting like sand, that waved back and forth on the road surface. Further along there had been a fresh fall that night, about two inches, and the plows had not yet cleared all the lanes. I was passing a Sunoco truck on a high curve when without warning the scraped section gave out and I realized I might skid into the fence if not over the edge. The radio was singing "Carpets of clover, I'll lay right at your feet," and the speedometer said 81. Nothing happened; the car stayed firm in the snow and Neil slept through the danger, his face turned skyward and his breath struggling in his nose. It was the first time I heard a contemporary of mine snore.

When we came into tunnel country the flicker and hollow amplification stirred Neil awake. He sat up, the mackinaw dropping to his lap, and lit a cigarette. A second after the scratch of his match occurred the moment of which each following moment was a slight diminution, as we made the long irregular descent toward Pittsburgh. There were many reasons for my feeling so happy. We were on our way. I had seen a dawn. This far, Neil could appreciate, I had brought us safely. Ahead, a girl waited who, if I asked, would marry me, but first there was a vast trip: many hours and towns interceded between me and that encounter. There was the quality of the 10 A.M. sunlight as it existed in the air ahead of the windshield, filtered by the thin overcast, blessing irresponsibility—you felt you could slice forever through such a cool pure element—and springing, by implying how high these hills had become, a widespreading pride: Pennsylvania, your state—as if you had made your life. And there was knowing that twice since midnight a person had trusted me enough to fall asleep beside me.

A Note on the Type

The text of this book was set on the Linotype in Janson, a recutting made direct from the type cast from matrices long thought to have been made by Anton Janson, a Dutchman who was a practising type-founder in Leipzig during the years 1668–1687. However, it has been conclusively demonstrated that these types are actually the work of Nicholas Kis (1650–1702) a Hungarian who learned his trade most probably from the master Dutch type-founder Dirk Voskens.

The type is an excellent example of the influential and sturdy Dutch types that prevailed in England prior to the development by William Caslon (1692–1766) of his own incomparable designs, which he evolved from these Dutch faces. The Dutch in their turn had been influenced by Claude Garamond (1510–1561) in France. The general tone of the Janson, however, is darker than Garamond and has a sturdiness and substance quite different from its predecessors.

The book was printed and bound by THE HADDON CRAFTSMEN, INC., *Scranton, Pennsylvania. Designed by Harry Ford.*

A Note About the Author

John Updike was born in 1932. He attended the Shillington, Pennsylvania, public schools, Harvard College, and the Ruskin School of Drawing and Fine Art, in Oxford, England. From 1955 to 1957 he was a member of the staff of *The New Yorker*, to which he has contributed short stories, many poems and some humor. In addition to his novels and story collections, he has published two books of poems, *The Carpentered Hen* (1958) and *Telephone Poles* (1963), and an adaptation of Mozart's opera *The Magic Flute* (1962). The author and his wife live in Ipswich, Massachusetts, with their four children.